Bully!

Also by Mark Schorr

Red Diamond: Private Eye
Ace of Diamonds
Diamond Rock

Bully!

Mark Schorr

St. Martin's Press
New York

BULLY! Copyright © 1985 by Mark Schorr. All rights reserved.
Printed in the United States of America. No part of this book may
be used or reproduced in any manner whatsoever without written
permission except in the case of brief quotations embodied in
critical articles or reviews. For information, address St. Martin's
Press, 175 Fifth Avenue, New York, N.Y. 10010.

Design by Doris Borowsky

Library of Congress Cataloging in Publication Data

Schorr, Mark.
  Bully!

  1. Roosevelt, Theodore, 1858–1919—Fiction.
I. Title.
PS3537.C598B8   1985   813'.52   85–12521
ISBN 0-312-01798-6

First Edition

10 9 8 7 6 5 4 3 2 1

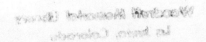

To Selly and Bill

Acknowledgments

I wish to thank the National Park Service rangers at Theodore Roosevelt's birthplace on East Twentieth Street in New York City, and at Sagamore Hill in Oyster Bay, Long Island, as well as Barbara Payne of the Public Inquiries office in Washington, D.C.

I would also like to acknowledge the contributions of librarians in the New York, Brooklyn, Los Angeles city and county public libraries, and the Long Island Historical Society.

My thanks to Marjorie Berg of the Magnificent Moorpark Melodrama and Vaudeville Company for her tips on turn-of-the-century theater, and Ron Ziel for sharing his knowledge of trains and TR.

Special thanks to the Theodore Roosevelt Association; its executive director, Dr. John Gable; and the numerous friends who provided anecdotes and sources as I researched this book.

The institutions and individuals who contributed their time and resources are heartily thanked for the many facts and accurate depictions of events in this book. For any errors or distortions, whether accidental or deliberate, I take full responsibility.

At the back of the book there is a partial bibliography for those who want to see where fact ends and fiction begins.

Preface

To most folks, President Theodore Roosevelt is nothing more than a head on Mount Rushmore, the Rough Rider who charged up San Juan hill and yelled "Bully!" all the time. Well, I can tell you he was a helluva lot more than that.

He's not the kind you can pigeonhole as a Democrat, Republican, liberal, conservative. He was for women's rights even though he grew up a proper Victorian. He was also the first president to invite a black to the White House and have a Jew in his Cabinet. He wasn't afraid of a fight, but he kept this country out of war, and was the first American to win the Nobel Peace Prize.

He was the first president to travel outside the country during office, to go in a submarine, and to fly in an airplane. And the only one to have a toy named after him.

But none of that has anything to do with the story I am about to tell. If you don't believe me, check the history books. Of course, you won't find *all* of it in the books. There's things I'm going to tell that have never been set down before.

So maybe some tales in here are on the tall side. If you want a textbook, go read one. If you want to find out about my buddy, Theodore Roosevelt, just keep turning the pages.

Bully!

one

The first time I saw Theodore Roosevelt was at the Snakebite Bar in 1884. It was the kind of place where they didn't water the liquor much, customers used the spittoons at least half the time, and no one got into fights they didn't think they could win.

There was nothing special about TR bellying up to the bullet-hole-pocked bar. He wasn't president. He was just a dude with big teeth, a bushy mustache, and round schoolmarm glasses. He was dressed the way Easterners imagined cowhands dressed: Stetson hat, fringed buckskin shirt, silk neckerchief, sealskin chaps, silver spurs on alligator boots. His Colt revolver had an ivory handle with his initials carved into it.

He was jabbering to the barkeep about the joys of "the strenuous life" and "good, clean, manly labor," not the sort of thing a wrangler loves to hear after a long day playing nursemaid to a few hundred tons of meat on the hoof. He had a way of talking that made it seem like he was biting into a chaw of tobacco with each word. And when he wasn't chomping, he was polishing his spectacles. You couldn't have missed him.

It was late afternoon and the Snakebite was packed tighter than a trough at feeding time. The crews from the Bar H, Triple Seven,

Running M, and Rocking R ranches were in town. I knew the Mingusville Jail would have a full house that night—everyone was putting it down pretty good.

But no one more than Kevin Clark, from the ranch over by Twin Forks Butte. He was a skinny, scrappy troublemaker who had come to the Badlands with the Northern Pacific Railroad and stayed on to become a fair to middling wrangler. Clark had hamhock hands and knuckles scraped raw from bar fights. The dust painting his clothes meant he had been stuck riding behind the herd again, and he was in a sour mood.

When Clark sidled over to TR, I knew there'd be trouble. I was playing five-card stud with a few pals. I was up fifty bucks and didn't want anything to disrupt the game.

"Hey, what are you drinking?" Clark demanded of Mr. Roosevelt, standing close enough that TR wrinkled his nose at the smell of cheap whiskey on Clark's breath.

"Brandy," Mr. Roosevelt said.

"What kind of sissy drink is that?"

Mr. Roosevelt ignored him and stared straight ahead at the mirror.

"Why don't you leave the customer alone," the barkeep said, nervously twiddling his mustache. He'd seen Clark in action and he wasn't eager to tangle with him.

"Me and Four Eyes is friends," Clark said. "Right?"

Mr. Roosevelt finished sipping his drink and turned to leave.

"Where you going, dude?" Clark demanded.

Mr. Roosevelt took a step away from the bar. Clark grabbed his shoulder.

"You hear me or you deaf too?"

"Let go," Mr. Roosevelt said. His voice was high-pitched, but it had a real strength to it.

The regulars sensed a showdown. Everyone had moved away from the two men. It got quiet.

"Four Eyes, you're gonna buy me and my pals a round to make up for being so rude," Clark said.

He shoved Mr. Roosevelt back toward the bar. Then the wrangler drew both his guns. Maybe he was thinking of making Mr. Roosevelt dance, maybe he just wanted to scare him.

I didn't see the first punch, a left that rocked Clark's head back. It was followed by a right hook that hit Clark like a mountain storm. He melted to the floor.

The wrangler's friends from Horse Nose Butte realized what was happening and took offense. A few of them began closing in on TR. I knew my game was going to be ruined—besides, the cards had gotten cold.

I stood with my six-gun at the ready. "Let's not be unsociable," I said.

I've got a bit of a reputation in town and the gang calmed down quick. They helped Clark off the sawdust and hurried out, muttering words that would make a mule-skinner blush.

"I'd like to buy you a drink," TR said with a boyish smile. He didn't seem at all frazzled by the near battle. I nodded, got a beer, and we walked to a table in back.

"My name is Theodore Roosevelt. I'm new to the area."

"I never woulda guessed."

He looked down at his clothing and chuckled. Right then, I knew I liked him. "Where'd you learn how to hit like that?" I asked.

"Harvard. I did rather well in amateur boxing."

"I didn't know they taught that kind of thing at East Coast fancy schools."

He chuckled again. "I was fortunate here. The surly gentleman stood too close and kept his feet together."

It was my turn to laugh. "That's probably the first time Clark's been called a gentleman of any sort."

3

We sized each other up. We both liked what we saw. He said he could use help at his Elkhorn Ranch.

"I can ride and rope anything that's got hair on it," I said. It may sound boastful now, but you've got to take into account I was eighteen at the time and full of piss and vinegar.

TR liked my attitude. He offered five dollars a week plus grub and a roof over my head. Needless to say, I accepted.

His spread covered seventy thousand acres where the Little Missouri River and Beaver Creek come together, near the western edge of the Dakota Territory. He had five thousand head of cattle.

The ranch house had eight rooms, a stone fireplace big enough to roast a cow, and even a photographic darkroom, where TR showed me how to make pictures. One wall in his den was covered with more books than I had ever seen.

My schooling wasn't anything to be ashamed of. I had been through all five volumes of *McGuffey's Reader* and knew the three *R*s as good as most.

But nothing like Mr. Roosevelt. When he wasn't working—which he did as hard as any man jack among us—he was writing a letter to someone or reading. The shelves were packed with books by Shakespeare, Irving, Hawthorne, Cooper, Franklin, and dozens of others. He let me borrow all I wanted, and was never too busy to talk about what a writer meant or why a character acted the way he did. "Books are as individual as friends," he said.

We became pretty good chums over the next couple of months, though we disagreed on quite a lot. He was a bit of a stuffed shirt. He wouldn't smoke a cigar, didn't drink much other than brandy or wine, and hated cussing or jokes about sex. He made a point of praising me for not joining the boys on their occasional trips to let off steam at Madame Anna's whorehouse over in Bismarck.

He had three favorite words that you couldn't go more than a few hours without hearing. One was "dee-lightful," which he said whenever he was happy, like when he shot his first bear. Another

4

was "manly." Above all else, he valued that in a companion, and I was mighty flattered that he considered me "quite a manly chap," as he told me a bunch of times. If he got excited over things going right, he would let out an explosive "Bully!"

When it was quiet and we were alone on the ranch, he would sometimes lower his guard.

"I was a rather sickly, rather timid little boy, very fond of desultory reading and of natural history and not excelling in any form of sport," he confessed one day. "Owing to my asthma I was not able to go to school and I was nervous and self-conscious. Not very manly, I would say."

His childhood asthma made him wheeze, spit up like a lung-er, and get out of breath real easy. But as he grew into his teens he overcame it and built himself up, lifting weights, hiking, and boxing.

"With proper character and determination a man can do just about anything," he explained.

Another time, it came out that a double heartache had led him out West. His wife had died on the same day as his mother. I could tell he loved them a great deal and talking about it made him very sad.

There were plenty of more pleasant topics to fill our conversations. We'd sit on the ranch veranda on the hot days, looking out at the cottonwoods, with me leaning against a pillar and TR in his rocker.

I grew up in Montana and figured I knew everything there was to know about the wild and what lived there. But he taught me a lot about things I took for granted. Where I saw a clump of rocks, he saw "a barren, fantastic, and grimly picturesque vista, with red scoria and veins of lignite." He told me how the petrified forest got there, about prehistoric swamps and monsters that ruled the earth.

I could look at an antelope dropping and tell the animal's size, whether it was in good health, and how long ago it had passed. He explained how it became an antelope and had me read a book by Charles Darwin. This evolution story was unbelievable, but it made for interesting conversations.

I had never been to a town bigger than Dickinson, which had a population of seven hundred. TR had been raised in New York City, gone to school in Boston, traveled in Europe, been a member of the New York State Assembly, and written a book on the Navy battles in the War of 1812.

He liked to talk and I liked to listen. We got along swell.

Some folks gave him a hard time at first. But he proved he could stand the gaff. Even when he got stuck on a trail ride on the meanest horse, he took the bouncing like a good sport.

He was even friendly with the Marquis de Mores—the founder of the cattle town of Medora—who scared hombres that could stare down a stampede. De Mores looked like the kind of villain you see in the nickelodeons tying sweet young things to the railroad tracks. He carried two Colts, a Winchester, and a Bowie knife strapped to his leg. He had killed two men in duels in France.

TR and the Marquis went over to Miles City to volunteer for a vigilante group going after rustlers. They were turned down because both of them were too well known. The rustlers were lucky.

A few years later the two gentlemen had a falling out that nearly resulted in a duel, but I only heard that secondhand. I don't intend to go spreading rumors.

I was with Mr. Roosevelt when he did get a chance to chase thieves, but they hadn't rustled cattle or horses. They were boat thieves.

We all knew how the boss felt about stealing.

Grant had been one of our best hands, but Mr. Roosevelt fired him on the spot when he saw him about to put an Elkhorn brand on a stray found on a neighbor's land. "A man who will steal *for* me will steal *from* me. You're fired," he said, chomping his teeth like there was no tomorrow.

So when TR heard about the boat being taken, he said, "To submit meekly to theft or any other injury is to invite repetition of the offense."

When he'd talk like that, I knew someday he was going to be in the limelight. He was already chairman of the Stockmen's Association, and a Billings County deputy sheriff. I thought he'd make a good governor, or senator when the Dakota Territories became a state. I guess I didn't think big enough.

The gunman we figured did it was a trigger-happy cattle rustler named Redhead Finnegan. He lived with two mean outlaws, making the pursuit a job for at least three good men.

A blizzard began to blow, the kind where the whole world turns white and howls and the devil tears at anything standing and throws it around like a rubber ball.

Mr. Roosevelt, who had no patience for anything or anybody that got in his way, insisted we take off after them before they got too much of a head start. Me and top hand Greg Braxton put together a makeshift boat. The future president, Braxton, and me set off in our boat on a fast-running river with an icy current. Braxton steered; TR and I watched for rocks that poked out of the water. TR said the rocks along the side reminded him of "the crouching figures of great goblin beasts." He took pictures.

That night the temperature was below zero. My teeth were chattering so loud I figured they'd be able to hear it in Rapid City. TR sat by the fire, reading a book called *Anna Karenina*. Roosevelt said the writer was Russian and the cold helped him enjoy it.

The next night, about a hundred miles downstream from where we started, we spotted the stolen skiff. We crept through the brush until we were a dozen yards away. Finnegan and his pals were huddled around a fire, warming their hands.

7

"If you move, I shall be forced to shoot," Mr. Roosevelt said, standing up and aiming his Winchester. Braxton and me, who had circled to outflank them, also stood, and the easy part of the chase was done.

TR wouldn't let us tie the varmints' hands or feet—he said the cold would cut off their blood supply. That meant we had to keep a watch on them at all times. We hit ice jams and ran low on food, but TR kept us going on with that enthusiasm of his.

At the foot of the Killdeer Mountains he pushed off alone and found a remote cow camp. Then he rode fifteen miles to the main ranch, where he got a team, wagon, and driver. He insisted on taking Finnegan and his buddies to the Dickinson sheriff. TR loaded the prisoners into the wagon while me and Braxton each took a boat and headed home.

Roosevelt walked forty-five miles to Dickinson, following the wagon with his Winchester at the ready. By the time he got to town, he hadn't slept for two days. The boat thieves got a stretch in the hoosegow, but I heard even they thought TR was quite a man.

When he went back East after a couple of years, I really hated to see him go. I was able to keep track of him through Medora's new newspaper, *The Bad Lands Cow Boy.* He ran for mayor of New York and lost, which I thought was a darn shame. He married a lady named Edith Carow, who he'd known since he was a kid, which I thought was very nice.

Mr. Roosevelt became a member of the Civil Service Commission in Washington and began getting rid of dead wood in government. He was the police commissioner of New York and made headlines by disguising himself and catching policemen goofing off. He became the Assistant Secretary of the Navy. The Spanish-American War got started.

I drifted around the country, riding the rails, taking odd jobs. I wound up in Chicago, working first in the stockyards and then for the Pinkertons. The pay was fair and catching crooks was fun. Then we started being used for strikebreaking, busting the heads of decent working folk who were doing nothing worse than struggling to put a little more bread on the table. I quit.

I wrote my ranchman boss. The letter I got back was as friendly as if we'd never been apart. He told me he was putting together a group of "manful men" who would set the Spaniards on their ear.

I went and joined him and he made me a sergeant right away. Teddy's Terrors, better known as the Rough Riders, were a strange mixture of his pals—East Coast fancy boys who talked funny, and Western knockabouts, like me, who had a talent for getting into jams. TR took the spoiled rich kids and the tough hombres and whipped them into a first-class fighting machine.

His adventures in Cuba have been told enough times. One thing that everyone doesn't know—Roosevelt's big moment wasn't on San Juan Hill. It was on Kettle Hill, where he was blooded, and killed a man face to face.

I remember the boom of the cannons, the clouds of smoke, and the zzzzzing of the Spanish Mausers. The snipers' high-speed bullets knocked a man down but often didn't kill. With tropical heat and wetness, the ailments that came from the wounds were meaner than the quick death of a clean shot.

The temperature was a hundred degrees. Sweat dripped off faster than we could pour water down our gullets. And most of the water we poured did unpleasant things to our bellies. The generals didn't know what to do and the bodies were piling up at Bloody Ford. The men began to talk about a retreat even though we could see the target, the Spanish blockhouse, only about a hundred yards ahead.

Between us and them was two rows of barbed wire and a never-ending stream of Mauser bullets. Mr. Roosevelt spurred Little Texas, a horse with as much heart as the future president, to the front. To men who hesitated, he shouted, "Are you afraid to stand when I am on horseback?"

I was right behind him as he stormed up the slope. The rest of the Rough Riders saw us move and the charge was on. Forty yards from the top we hit the second barbed-wire line and Little Texas balked. Without losing momentum, TR jumped from his mount and hopped the fence. A bullet grazed his elbow. The Rough Riders gave us covering fire, and Spaniards popped out of the house like rats deserting a sinking ship.

Then one stood there, his rifle trained on Colonel Theodore Roosevelt. It was hotter than hell but time froze.

TR lifted the revolver he carried, a five-shot Navy pistol salvaged from the sunken *Maine*. Before the Spanish soldier could squeeze the trigger, Colonel Roosevelt had hit him square in the middle, folding him over.

The Spanish lost their will to fight after seeing our leader, who their man had dead to rights, once again escape death. TR and me paused at the top of Kettle Hill, out of breath, watching fleeing Spaniards and General Kent's men charging neighboring San Juan Hill. We gave them covering fire, and you know what the outcome was.

In a quiet moment, I saw the colonel over by the soldier he'd killed. The dead man's eyes had rolled and flies were buzzing the fatal wound. The soldier was no older than twenty and he probably didn't need to shave more than once a week. TR's mouth was puckered and his eyes were more squinty than usual.

"How you doing, sir?" I asked.

He nodded.

"The first time you killed a man?"

He nodded again and turned to me with glittery, moist eyes. I couldn't tell if he was excited or about to cry.

"All men who feel any joy in battle know what it is like when the wolf rises in the heart," he said.

10

"Sir?"

"I feel I've touched an unholy animal spirit within me. I've always wondered what it would be like to kill a man. Now I know, and I wish I had never learned." He sighed, rubbed his sweat-fogged spectacles furiously, and then clapped me on the back. "Let's go win this war, Jim."

And we did.

At our mustering out in Montauk three months later, the troops presented him with a Frederic Remington bronze of a bronco-buster. Mr. Roosevelt was never at a loss for words, but he just stood silent in front of the nine hundred men of the First Volunteer Cavalry, stroking the bronze bronco's mane. He finally began speaking in the high-pitched voice that we had come to love:

"Nothing could possibly happen that would touch and please me as much as this," he said, chomping each word as he petted the statuette. "It comes to me from you who endured the hardships of the campaign with me, who shared your hardtack when I had none, and who gave me your blankets when I had none to lie upon. To have such a gift come from this regiment touches me more than I can say."

He recalled battles we had been in, the buddies we had seen die, the wounds we would carry for the rest of our lives.

"We are *all* Americans," he said. "Americanism means the virtues of courage, honor, justice, sincerity, and hardihood—the virtues that made America."

By the time he was done, we were crying the way we had been sweating in the forests of Cuba.

I went back West, and saw the land ruined by dudes, bankers, and businessmen who would tear down a forest to put up an outhouse. Every day the frontier got a little smaller. I decided to try my fortune in the city. I rode the rails back to Chicago and married a pretty Italian gal.

After six very happy months she came down with consumption and spent days moaning in pain. It tore me up more than I'd like to admit. I felt so helpless. When she died, I guess I went a bit out of my head.

I don't recall the better part of two years. Somehow I found myself working as a trainer at the Gravesend Race Track in Brooklyn.

Mr. Roosevelt became governor and then vice-president. One day, I decided to write a letter to congratulate him. I sent a quick note and gave my address, a small bungalow near Kings Highway in Brooklyn.

He wrote back. That's the kind of fella he was, the vice-president, and he'd write back like we were equals. He told how he hadn't really wanted the job. He'd been swept along by friends who saw him as a future presidential candidate, and by foes eager to get him out of power in New York. He invited me to Washington.

My own lying got in my way. I had made it seem in my letter like I was doing much better than I was. I couldn't bring myself to face him and tell him the truth. I didn't write back.

The stable I was working at went out of business. Because of the hard times in the country I couldn't get a new job. The bank foreclosed on my mortgage. I wound up in a fleabag hotel in Coney Island. The new century started and it didn't look promising for me. I was thirty-five and lucky to get work as a stable boy.

Then McKinley got shot and my old boss became the twenty-sixth president of the United States.

One morning a burly man who said he was William Craig of the United States Secret Service came knocking at my door. It wasn't the first time a law-enforcement officer had come for someone at the hotel. The geezer behind the front desk was only concerned that my rent was paid up. Craig insisted I go with him. No cuffs were put on me and he called me "Mr. White," so I had a feeling I wasn't in trouble. After a few attempts, I gave up asking him what was going on.

He took me to the Flatbush Avenue Long Island Railroad train station, bought us tickets, and we went for a ride out to Oyster Bay.

The livery man was real respectful as he handed over a plain black buckboard. Craig and I climbed aboard, he gave the horses a whip, and we took off. I noticed a shotgun across the floor of the buggy, hidden from view, but within easy reach.

It was beautiful country, not at all like the overcrowded neighborhoods where I had been living. I was thinking about taking a trip West when we pulled off on a private road and a three-story house came into view. The first story was a reddish brick, with green trim shutters and pillars on the porch. The top two stories were wood painted the color of mustard. There were deers' antlers at the peak of a couple of the gables.

But we didn't go to the house, turning instead to follow a dirt road that led down to near Long Island Sound. Craig stopped the buggy and got out. "Wait here," he ordered. He had friendly blue eyes, but a no-nonsense manner.

I hadn't realized how much I missed the country. I was drinking up the view the way I used to drink rotgut when I heard a voice behind me shout "Bully!" and I knew who had brought me back to nature.

"Colonel Roosevelt, I mean, Mr. President, sir."

"One or the other, no need for both," he said, barreling out of the woods and pumping my hand. "You've lost weight. I wish I could say the same." He patted his belly, which had gotten bigger, though he still looked fit enough to wrestle a grizzly.

I smiled. "Sir, I'm pleased to see you, but if you don't mind my saying so, I'm confused. Don't get me wrong, I'm honored to see you again. But I didn't even get a chance to shave." I rubbed my stubbly chin, feeling bad about the patches on my pants and the worn spots on my jacket.

"I apologize for the urgent summons," he said, taking off his glasses and giving them the wipes I remembered so well. "Jim, I'm in trouble and need your help."

two

"Walk with me, Jim," he said. I followed him into the grove of birch trees. "You'll understand my irregular method of summoning you after I explain what happened to me. First, however, I want to hear what you have been doing since we were mustered out at Montauk."

I was going to tell him a tall tale, but I knew how he hated humbuggery. I told him what had happened as we walked.

His questions were all fair, with none of the looking down the nose you might expect from a president talking to an ordinary joe. He nodded along, showing no signs of surprise. I felt he knew everything even before I opened my mouth.

As we walked I could see guards posted in the distance watching us carefully. He noticed me eyeing them.

"Do you recall that song, 'A Bird In A Gilded Cage'?" Roosevelt asked. "My protectors are my jailers. The Secret Servicemen follow me like goslings behind their mother, fearing I'll wind up like McKinley. It has almost gotten to the point of a game, where I sneak off to enjoy a few moments of privacy. Of course, it was going off on my own that got me into the terrible fix I currently find myself in."

15

During our brisk stroll through waist-high grass, flocks of swallows, finches, sparrows, orioles, and robins serenaded us. He told me he had counted forty-two types of birds around his home, and began reciting them.

"There goes a red-eyed vireo, known as *vireo olnaceus,*" he said. "That small basketlike cup in the black locust tree, known more precisely as *robinia pseudoacacia,* is its home. The vireos sound like robins, with . . ."

I didn't have to be an ex-Pinkerton to figure out that I hadn't been contacted just for a lecture on bird-watching.

"It's not fair to keep a grown man cooped up in a house like a sick child," he finally said. "With all the tribulations of the presidency, it's only natural to yearn to escape the Executive Mansion."

He reached down, pulled up a rush, and twisted it between his stubby fingers. When it was completely shredded, he said, "James, what I am about to tell you is a matter of the gravest significance, not only to myself, but to this nation as a whole. I ask that you swear an oath of absolute secrecy. The story must not be released to the American public while I am alive."

"It will go no further," I said, solemnly raising my right hand.

"I know I can trust you. That is why you were brought here. There are not many men whom I trust to keep their own counsel and act in a manly way. As this nation's leader, I must be especially careful."

"I give you my word, Mr. President."

He then told me the tale of woe that was tearing at him like a hungry mountain lion.

At the end of a hectic day, the president would slip out of the back door of the White House and go for a half-hour run around the Washington Monument and neighboring streets. It was a might strange, a grown man running if he wasn't being chased, but he found it helped clear his head. He kept a hat pulled low, and during the winter, a scarf over his face to avoid drawing attention. The newspapers had had enough fun with stories of him practicing his boxing with champions who visited the White House.

It was a blustery October night, four days earlier, near the house where Lincoln had died, when the incident occurred. A young blind woman was tapping her way along E Street. She was well dressed, with a woolen shawl across her frail shoulders. Her eyes were covered by round spectacles with black glass.

TR was admiring her spunk as she made her way down the deserted street when he saw two men watching her. They were in their thirties, shabbily dressed, waiting like buzzards for a meal. The hooligans attacked, knocking her down and grabbing her silk purse. She fell in the gutter, nearly landing in a pile of horse droppings. TR planned to chase the bandits, but the lady moaned and he decided she needed his attention.

"Are you all right?" he asked.

"Oh yes, I'm fine," she said, in a voice full of good breeding. Her hat had blown away. He retrieved her cane and helped her up.

"I'll call a policeman to snare those villians," he told her.

"Please do not bother," she said formally. "There wasn't much in my purse. It isn't necessary to trouble the constabulary. I'll be on my way." She took a few steps and swooned. He caught her in his arms.

"Oh, I am so sorry," she said, righting herself. "Please forgive me."

"There's nothing to forgive, madam. Allow me to call you a hansom cab."

"I'm already in your debt. Who knows what those men would've tried if you hadn't happened along."

TR harrumphed modestly.

"I live only around the corner," she said. "I don't need a cab. But, if I might dare. . . ?"

"Yes?"

17

"Would you be willing to escort me? In case the ruffians are still in the area."

"I would be honored."

He walked with her, a foot or so away and nearer to the curb. As he kept alert for any threat, she told her story.

Her name was Minnie Adams. Twenty years old, originally from Indiana, she had worked in a New Jersey hat factory until a mercury spill blinded her. Now she lived with her mother and took in piecework, doing sewing by touch.

"My wife might be able to use your services," Mr. Roosevelt said. "I'll mention you to her."

"You are too kind. Tell me about yourself."

It was a quirky joy, being with someone who had no idea who he was. He described himself only as a civil servant and stuck to tales of his family life.

Then they were at her home, a well-kept townhouse indistinguishable from its neighbors.

"Will you come in, kind sir?"

"I must be getting on."

"Please. Just to say hello to my mother. She would be sad if she didn't have a chance to thank you personally."

"Well, only for a moment," he said, pulling his scarf up and his hat down. They walked downstairs to her basement apartment. A light was on inside and TR saw a figure moving in the kitchen.

Minnie fumbled with the key as she opened the door. They stepped inside and she shut the door behind them. She swooned again and he caught her. While her legs collapsed, she dropped her shawl and glasses, knocked aside his hat and scarf, and tore the top of her own dress, baring a milky-white shoulder.

At that moment, one of the purse-snatchers appeared from the kitchen with a camera in his hand. The flash stunned TR. Despite the surprise, Mr. Roosevelt's reflexes were quick. He brushed aside his chivalry, and the woman.

"Bastard," she growled, quickly regaining her balance.

Mr. Roosevelt charged the man with the camera and they grappled fiercely. The photographer was a tough ruffian, but no match for a man who enjoyed sparring with the likes of John L. Sullivan, Battling Nelson, and Bob Fitzsimmons.

The second purse-snatcher jumped from a hiding place. They pounded TR while Minnie cheered. Roosevelt fought with all his vigor and the tide turned. One of them drew a pistol and ordered, "Don't move!"

Mr. Roosevelt answered with a right cross at the same time the villain squeezed the trigger. Three shots went wild before TR's fists sent him crashing into his accomplice. Both men toppled over the table. TR grabbed the camera.

"Oh my God!" one of the men said.

The woman who had called herself Minnie Adams would fake swoons no more. She lay on the floor, an ugly patch of blood staining the front of her dress. TR heard the movement behind him, but by the time he turned, the men were gone. He was alone with the dead woman. He knelt and checked her pulse even though he knew it was pointless.

How could the president prove that he had not fired the fatal bullet? In his own hands he held a damning piece of evidence, a camera with a plate showing him and the woman embracing. Or was he a masher trying to have his way? Either way the scandal sheets would have a field day. His achievements would be forgotten, his name dragged through the mud. Edith and his six children wouldn't be able to hold their heads up anywhere in the civilized world.

With the camera under his coat, TR fled, leaving Minnie Adams' corpse staring at the ceiling. He had to walk slowly, finding it hard to breathe. The asthma he had battled since his youth was choking him. He made it to the White House and hid the camera.

"With the Secret Service shadowing me, and various and sundry affairs of state taking up my time, I cannot handle this matter alone."

"So you want me to look into it, see who was trying to embarrass you?" I asked.

"The first thing to ascertain is if I was indeed the target of the conspirators. I may have stumbled onto a blackmail scheme meant for another. The streets of Washington are populated by numerous dignitaries."

"But what happens then? What happens once we find the blackmailers?"

"As president, I cannot allow myself to be linked to any such scandal, no matter how properly I may have conducted myself. My fleeing the scene implies a certain culpability. I'll figure out a solution that assures justice is done and does not hinder my work. Will you help?"

"There's never been any question."

"Bully!" he said, and clapped me on the shoulder.

He had chosen that day to contact me because his family was on an overnight visit at a relative's house. We would have more time to speak privately without the sizable Roosevelt brood galloping about.

The first face to greet me as we stepped into the twenty-three-room house belonged to a buffalo. The shaggy trophy, along with two deer heads, stared down from above the fireplace in the oak-paneled entrance hall. Off to the right, where he had southern exposure and a view of anyone coming up the road, was Mr. Roosevelt's library.

He had even more books than he'd had at Elkhorn. There were pictures of his relatives, including a large portrait of TR's com-

manding-looking father, mounted animal heads, a chest-high fireplace, animal skins on the floor. He had an oak desk, pine rocking
chairs, and an eight-bell chime on the mahogany mantelpiece. The
broncobuster bronze by Remington sat in a place of honor on the
mantel and brought back memories.

Off to the left was the drawing room, much lighter in color. It
was white and robin's-egg blue, with porcelains and finely woven
rugs. He didn't need to tell me this was where the lady of the
house held court.

"You'll see the rest of Sagamore Hill," TR said, and briskly took
off up the stairs. As I was about to climb, I noticed a comely
young woman watching me from the kitchen. She wore a maid's
black-and-white outfit and a mischievous smile on her pretty,
freckled face. She was about thirty years old, with bright red hair
peeking out from under her bonnet.

Mr. Roosevelt was already at the top of the landing. "Come on,
Jim, no dawdling," he boomed and was off. The woman disappeared into the kitchen and I hurried up the stairs.

The second floor had bedrooms, a bathroom, the nursery and
dressing room. I wanted to snoop around—I don't expect anyone
wouldn't be curious to see how a president actually lives. On the
walls were portraits of Colonel Theodore Roosevelt, two of his
sons, Archie and Quentin, and an etching of Davy Crockett. I
didn't have time to admire the artwork, for TR was already pacing
around upstairs and I knew he'd be straining at the bit if I gawked
more than a few seconds.

He was waiting for me in a west-facing room right under the
sloped roof. Through the windows, you could see the sunlight
shining off Long Island Sound and, in the distance, the green Con-
necticut shore.

"My Gun Room," he said, and by the way he did I could tell I
was in his favorite spot. He had a desk, wooden bow chairs, a
cushioned horsehair chair, and a cabinet packed with the weapons.

On the white walls were enough firearms to fill an armory. There were more animal skins and heads, and a small revolving bookcase. On his desk he had one of those new typewriting gadgets and piles of papers.

TR shut the door behind us and walked to the fireplace. His normally animated features grew somber. He reached into the flue and took down a photograph, handling it like it was both precious and deadly.

It was a woman, pretty as a Gibson girl, being held in a man's arms. The president had cut his own image out of the picture, but still it was as dangerous as a stick of TNT. Her full lips were open, giving her a shocked expression. Her dark hair was mussed.

"Take it. It will be needed during the investigation," he said.

I pocketed the photograph. "Was her death written up in the newspapers?"

He went to his desk and dug out a few clippings from *The Washington Post and The Washington Evening Star*. They said that a woman named Margaret Anders, twenty-four years of age, was found dead in an apartment whose owners were vacationing on Chesapeake Bay. Police said the elderly couple who lived there had no connection with the dead woman. Someone had broken out the original locks, and replaced them with ones to which Anders held the key. Margaret Anders, the report noted, was an actress who hailed from the city of Brooklyn—now part of greater New York City. Her reason for being in the residence remained a mystery.

TR had taken a revolver off the wall and was fiddling with it when I finished. "How much are you earning now?" he asked.

"Ten dollars a week."

"Would sixty dollars a week be fair?"

"More than fair."

"You will let me know of any expenses. Since this is a personal matter, your payment will be drawn from my own funds. Edith manages our finances, so it might take a little scrimping on my part before you receive payment."

"Your marker is good with me, sir."

He smiled at my response, but I could see his thoughts were elsewhere. "She is a tough taskmistress, nevertheless I am sure you will get along splendidly."

"I met Mrs. Roosevelt at Montauk when we were mustered out," I said. "She is a fine lady."

"Isn't she?" he asked in a reverential tone. He stood by the window. The sun had gone down a few degrees and was turning orange as it neared the surface of Long Island Sound. The president stared at the flaming ball. "I care as much about hurting her and the children as the effect this scandal would have on the nation. They are the only things in this world I love more than the presidency, more than life itself." He turned to me. "You must be careful to keep your reason for being here from them."

"What should I tell them?"

"Many former Rough Riders have corresponded with me and a few have visited previously," he said, putting the gun back on the wall. "I believe you are about the same size as Bill Craig. He's the stout-hearted fellow who brought you here. I am sure he can loan you some fit apparel."

"By the way, who was that young lady we passed on the way up here?"

"Audrey McFarlane. She's been our maid for six years. Why do you ask?"

"Merely curious."

Before leaving the Gun Room, he handed me six gold ten-dollar pieces. They felt comfortable in my pocket though I felt bad accepting them. How many men could claim the honor of working as a confidential agent for the president of the United States, more trusted than the whole Pinkerton organization or his own Secret Service? I didn't feel bad enough to return them, however.

three

TR was sitting in his library, writing at the big desk under the portrait of his father. "Come in, come in," he said when he looked up and noticed me. "Have you made yourself at home?"

"Almost."

"Supper is at seven. Be at the table promptly, or our cook, Annie O'Rourke, will box your ears. She fussed about having an unexpected plate to set, but I do believe she always enjoys having someone new to badger. Oh, that reminds me, have you seen a badger running about?"

"I didn't walk very far," I confessed.

"No, not outside. In the house."

"I can't say I have."

"If you do, give me a call. His name is Josiah. He's my son Archie's, and the little scamp didn't lock him up before leaving. Josiah is fundamentally friendly, although he does have a short temper and sharp teeth."

"I'll be on my guard."

"I picked him up during my trip West this spring. I had a most outstanding guide during my exploration of California, John Muir. You would like him. Seeing the forests with him is like viewing a new sight with a child. A grove of giant redwood or sequoias should be kept just as we keep a great and beautiful cathedral. Short-sighted loggers must be reined in."

"How can you protect the trees?"

"With an act of Congress they can be made into a national park. My party will have a substantial majority in the Senate and the House when the fifty-eighth session of Congress commences next week. Sometimes, however, the legislators move too slowly, or they receive pressure, and perhaps other things, from those for whom a sawmill is more attractive than a grove of trees. As president, I can declare the site a national monument. That keeps those greedy scoundrels from defiling the landscape."

There was a scuttling noise in the hall and TR was up in a flash, moving with a speed that gave the lie to his stocky figure. "Josiah!" he shouted before hurrying out of the room.

I couldn't resist snooping. I took a peek at the president's letter. It was to his son and namesake, who was a student at Groton: "Remember how great Lincoln was, try to be as patient and uncomplaining as well as resolute as Lincoln in dealing not only with knaves but with the well-meaning foolish people, educated and uneducated, who give the knaves their chance," TR had written.

The president came back into the room. If he saw me reading, he didn't say. "It wasn't him."

"What was it?"

"Jack chasing Tom Quartz, who was after Bishop Doane."

"What?" I exclaimed.

"Jack, the terrier, was pursuing the kitten, Tom Quartz, who was after the guinea pig, Bishop Doane."

"The pets have unusual names."

He chuckled. "I won't even try and remember the names of all the rabbits. Let's see, there's Eli, the macaw; Bill, the lizard; Admiral Dewey and Fighting Bob Evans, who are also guinea pigs; and Algonquin, the pony. I must tell you about the time Archie was ill and Quentin smuggled the pony into his bedroom in the White House."

"How did he do that?"

"By elevator. Algonquin was quite manageable once he discovered his reflection in the mirror." TR picked up the letter to his son and grew serious. "I hope I am not too stern with the boy. I know I used to be."

"I'm sure you're not, sir."

He folded the letter and put it in an envelope. "We better get ready for dinner."

McFarlane was pouring hot water into a large metal tub she had set on the floor of the guest room. I was going to offer my help, but wondered what the etiquette was. It wasn't every day I was waited on by servants. So all I did was admire her slender but womanly figure.

"You can be shaving while I finish here," McFarlane said. She bent to adjust the tub, giving me a view of a very well-turned ankle. She saw me looking.

"Do you like what you see?" she said challengingly.

"You are a saucy one, aren't you?" There was a tension as great as one of Mr. Edison's electric charges between us. I left to freshen up before we lit up the room.

As I dipped the lathering brush into the china mug with the Roosevelt family crest—three red roses growing out of a green bush on a gray background—I felt a wave of excitement. I was in the home of the president of the United States, trimming my whiskers with a straight razor that might very well have shaved that famous face.

Audrey was gone when I got back to the guest room. I locked the door, peeled off my clothes, and slid into an almost unbearably hot tub. It was great. I closed my eyes and daydreamed. I thought of the letter from the president to his son. It made me jealous of young Teddy. My own Pa never learned how to sign more than an X, and he was too busy bringing home the bacon to talk much.

But I didn't have time to feel sorry for myself. And what kind of person would sit in the president's bathtub and complain about the hand Fate had dealt him?

I began thinking about the case before me. Being partial to those new books by Arthur Conan Doyle about the British detective with uncanny powers of observation, I had a daydream where I solved the problem, and said, "Elementary, my dear Roosevelt."

Dinner was a humdinger: broiled chicken in lemon sauce, with carrots and peas, and chicken gravy over rice. Hovering around the table was Annie O'Rourke, a chunky woman who reminded me of a mother hen. McFarlane did most of the serving. Once or twice she accidently brushed against me. Again I felt that electricity.

I made a point of talking about the problem only when the servants were out of the room. "This habit of running around the Washington Monument, for how long have you been doing it?" I asked when we were alone.

"Since I became president."

"How many people know about it?"

"My family, my immediate staff. No one else. Why? Wait, I see. If the hoodlums had me in mind as their victim, someone had to tip them off to my schedule. But that means someone I have allowed to become close to me has betrayed me.

"Impossible," he said after a pause. There was another long pause. He was silent and suffering. I had seen that look before. When I was a Pinkerton, I caught an Ohio banker embezzling money from his father-in-law's company. The old man wished I hadn't found the culprit.

"It could be a federal employee, someone who doesn't know you personally," I suggested.

"That would be more likely. But who could it be?"

Audrey came in and checked that everything was okay. I said it was the best meal I had had in years, which was true. The president chewed his food like it was old straw.

"How come you're here and not in Washington?" I asked, trying to distract him.

"Returning to Sagamore revitalizes me. It's necessary to breathe fresh air after the miasma of politicians and their ilk. I think they chose to build our capitol on a swamp so those reptiles would feel at home."

The cook came into the room, saw we had cleaned our plates, and fetched a bowl of chocolate pudding with whipped cream. Mr. Roosevelt insisted he was full, but she overwhelmed us, and we dug in. As soon as my spoon touched the bottom of the bowl O'Rourke appeared and refilled it. I could see how Mr. Roosevelt picked up the extra baggage on his frame.

"Mr. President, a plot involving a break-in, an actress, armed men, and a camera is a sophisticated one," I said when we were alone again.

"You are correct, Jim, and the obvious conclusion is that they were professionals who caught the mark they had in mind," he said. "I have been denying it to myself." The president got up. "Would you like to get a breath of fresh air?"

We walked out to the veranda and sat in rocking chairs. We could see the running lights of boats on Long Island Sound and hear their horns. A cool night breeze was blowing off the water. TR took off his glasses, buffed them, and rocked back and forth.

"Assuming I was indeed the target, how would you go about investigating the matter?"

"Mr. Pinkerton always said the easiest way to investigate is to start with the persons who might have a motive and cross them off the list until you are left with one or two likely suspects. Then surveillance and other techniques nail the lid down."

"There are two major problems. The first is that the utmost discretion is required. Any action that could reveal my involvement must be avoided at all costs."

"Can you wait for them to make the next move?"

"I despise playing from a defensive position," he said.

"You mentioned a second problem?"

"Examining the list of those who bear me malice is a Herculean chore. I have never been afraid to make an enemy or fight for a friend."

"But who would have the resources to have you bushwhacked and blackmailed?"

"I stepped on the toes of many a corrupt police official," he said with a chuckle. "The Tammany Hall blackguards never forgave me for the way I dealt with them while I was assemblyman and governor."

He began pacing.

"Every robber baron wishes me ill. The Ku Klux Klan named me as their number one enemy after I invited Booker T. Washington to the White House."

His feet echoed on the wooden floor.

"Numerous foreign governments have been upset with my diplomatic policies. Powers in my own party would be happy if I were to fall from grace with a thud."

He chomped out his words.

"There's also the lunatic fringe. Just last week, the Secret Service apprehended a man with a dagger who was halfway to my office. During my uncle's funeral, a man began ranting and blaming me for Kaiser Wilhelm's illness." TR snorted. "At least we can probably rule them out. The scheme was too well organized and funded to be the work of a deranged mind. Anyway, you can see that the list of my adversaries is quite lengthy."

"The list of your friends would be much larger."

"Thank you. I am glad you are on that list."

"Of all the skunks, who's giving you the most trouble right now?"

"That varies from minute to minute. For example, have you been following the coal strike?"

"A bit."

"George Baer of the Reading Railroad believes he's being guided by God! He says decent Christian workingmen should accept his word as if it came from on high. And Crittenden. He has coal mines, a railroad, a newspaper, and acres of woodland. He doesn't have as much money as J.P. Morgan, but he's at least as arrogant. He insisted I shouldn't yield my principles and agree to arbitration with the miners.

"As if he knows my principles! He said he would be willing to suffer through the winter in the event of a shortage. For him that might mean shutting down a few of the twenty-five rooms in his mansion on Park Avenue or his house in Newport. It wouldn't mean spending winter huddled under a blanket in an apartment where the temperature never rises above thirty degrees.

"Child labor is a national disgrace, but nowhere is it more of an abomination than in Crittenden's mines and factories. The small bodies fit so well into tight holes. He does not care if they never come out, if they lose life and limb in the bowels of the earth."

He ranted on about Andrew Carnegie, E.H. Harriman, and others. His face got red and he pounded his fist into his open palm. He told me about Standard Oil Company. Rockefeller was fighting the government tooth and nail over every regulatory statute passed. The oil magnate had gotten it into his head that the government should not control the giant corporations in any way.

"Who else but the federal government is large enough to challenge these men and their corporations? If I were unable to combat them, they would fell every tree, mine every inch of earth, fill the sky with smoke, and reduce wages to a pittance. They are malefactors of wealth, with no thought for the dignity of man or the planet they plunder. If they had their way, the vast majority would do nothing more than toil and die so these few could grow even fatter and richer."

The president was off and rolling. I don't think I got in more than a dozen words the rest of the night, and they were all just agreeing with him.

"Frankly, I don't know if even the president can control these monster corporations," TR said. "They are governments unto themselves. They have evolved like savage predatory beasts, survival of the fittest, which has given us the most selfish, ruthless, and dangerous captains of industry emerging triumphant." He had thrown down the gauntlet with the Antitrust Act six months ago, and at first the robber barons merely scoffed. Then they saw he was serious.

"They try and brand me a socialist because I will not let them run rampant. What these fools don't understand is that this isn't the nineteenth century anymore. These United States will not be a good place for any of us to live in if it is not a reasonably good place for all of us to live in."

He paused to get some air. "The Democrats say I am tough on big business only to blackmail money for the 1904 campaign. What they do not know, and I presume you will keep to yourself, is that there is a good chance I will not run."

"What?"

"Do you know that no vice-president who ever filled out a president's term has been elected to that office? And I am the youngest man ever to ascend to the White House. The working man sees me as a rich man's son, a tool of the Trusts. The robber barons see me as the greatest threat since the trade unions. My own party considers me a mugwump. But I am not complaining. I wouldn't trade one moment of it, not one moment of it." He paused again to recharge, then thought the better of it.

Talk drifted to what had become of acquaintances from the Badlands and the Rough Riders. I gave him details of the sad life of Tom Horn, who was waiting to be hanged in Cheyenne. He told me of the adventures of Marquis de Mores, who had failed at a bunch of businesses and gone to Africa. In the Sahara he was way-laid by a gang of bandits. He took a dozen cutthroats with him to the grave.

He also brought me up to date on the exploits of General Leonard Wood. Wood had already been a Congressional Medal of Honor winner—awarded after an 1886 campaign against the Apaches—when he commanded the Rough Riders. McKinley had made him military governor of Cuba. Wood, a doctor, had done good things in the battle against tropical diseases. TR planned to send him to the Philippines.

I was never as fond of Wood as Mr. Roosevelt was. The general was a top-notch military man, but he had all the warmth and kindness of a cocked Winchester. It was good to know he was on our side, and equally as pleasing to know he was soon going several thousand miles away. I did not envy the Filipinos.

We went to the library, where we sipped brandy and TR lectured long into the night. He could jump easily from an argument in favor of the gold standard, to how brandy came about from French winemakers being forced to ship wine extracts to Holland during the Thirty Years' War, to how little creatures smaller than bugs actually caused most sicknesses.

He was without a doubt the smartest man I knew.

I left him reading in the library as the clock neared midnight, and that was the way I found him the next morning, though he had gone from the poems of Browning to government business. He held up a stack of letters from cabinet members, congressmen, and citizens. "Since you have a great interest in my mail, would you care to see these?"

"Uh, no sir. I'm sorry if it seemed that—"

"That's all right. One day all my correspondence will probably turn up in some scandalmongering rag like *Town Topics,* to show the American public how dull their president is. Have you had breakfast?"

I patted a very full belly.

"Bully. Let us be off then."

"Us?"

"Yes. I would not let you go off alone on this adventure."

"But sir, whoever is behind this already tried to get you. I'd feel terrible, and you'd feel even worse if—"

"I will brook no objections. We must be off," he said, getting up from behind his desk. "I have our route planned out."

"Everybody knows what you look like," I protested.

"That can work to my advantage. I have been reading up on the subject, a fascinating treatise by an inspector with Scotland Yard's Special Branch." I followed at a near run as he bounded up the stairs like a little boy. "I have a distinct advantage in assuming a disguise, in that my features *are* so well known. Say Roosevelt, and the average person immediately pictures a very definite image."

We were in the Gun Room and he shut the door. He took out mustache wax, tinted hair tonic, a black pince-nez, a derby, and a pillow with bands of fabric attached.

"Do you know when I was police commissioner, I once received a letter that had no name or number, only a crude drawing of a pair of spectacles, mustache, and teeth?" he asked as he strapped the pillow around his waist. Facing the mirror, he waxed his mustache down and slicked his hair. "Still, while commissioner, I was able to lurk about town in disguise, catching shirkers and malingerers in the act.

"The hairline and shape of the head are actually the way we most easily recognize others," he said. "Did you know that?"

I told him I didn't and tried harder to convince him to stay back and mind the fort, but he continued preparing. "You are the president. What happens if you should be injured?"

"Only those are fit to live who do not fear to die," he said. He replaced his glasses with the pince-nez and pulled on the hat. "Whatever I think is right for me to do, I do. When I make up my mind to do a thing, I act."

The change was remarkable. He admired himself in the mirror.

"Where do you want to start?" he asked.

"She came from Brooklyn. We might as well be on familiar turf."

"Let the hunt begin."

four

After sneaking to a buckboard that TR had stashed in the woods, we rode to the Long Island Railroad station and then caught a train into the city.

We began our snooping by going from theater to theater, speaking to porters, box-office clerks, stage managers, actors and actresses, and showing the photograph.

"It feels grand to be back in action. Like the old days, right Jim?" TR said after fruitless stops at entertainment houses in the downtown Brooklyn area.

"Uh-huh," I said halfheartedly. TR was a good man to have around in a pinch, but I felt like I was leading the future of America into the mouth of a lion.

At each stop, I recited a sob story, telling how the woman in the photograph was our little sister, our mother was dying and wanted to see her before she went to meet her Maker. I don't know whether they believed me, but they certainly enjoyed my performance. I sweetened the show by offering a ten-dollar gold piece to anyone who could give information.

It wasn't until we reached the Grand Opera House on Elm Place that we met with luck. The front of the theater was covered by a large porch, which featured all sorts of flowery gingerbread woodworking. Despite its name, no fancy Italian singers ever strained their vocal cords there. It was a showplace only for second-rate vaudeville acts.

We showed the picture of the woman to the cheroot-chewing man in the box office. He said he'd never seen her. But he said it too quickly and then looked away nervously.

"I think we may be on to something here," TR whispered to me. We bought tickets and moseyed in, finding seats toward the front of the theater.

A scarecrow-skinny man walked out on stage with a banana in his ear. Another man tried long and hard to tell him he had a banana in his ear. Finally, the skinny man said, "I am truly sorry I cannot hear you, as I have a banana in my ear."

The all-male audience, which about half-filled the theater, laughed loudly. Then the dance-hall girls were brought out. The crowd roared during a performance of "In the Good Old Summertime," where women in daring linen bathing suits frolicked on a make-believe beach.

The president harrumphed, then whispered to me, "I'll go backstage." He got up.

"Siddown, Fatso!" a nearby man with a gallaway beard yelled. "And take your hat off."

The president clenched his fists, but controlled his temper, removed his hat, and double-timed down the aisle. I followed.

Our way backstage was blocked by a giant with massive muttonchops covering a good portion of his face and not one hair on top of his head. He had arms as thick as tree trunks, folded across a gigantic chest.

"Perhaps you can help me," I said, launching into my tale of woe. The guard, who must have topped six-and-a-half feet, didn't change his expression or look at my photograph.

"Skedaddle," he barked.

"Oh, Zach, don't be so hard on them," a woman behind him said.

To describe her as a woman is an understatement. She was a voluptuous hourglass in a bodice, with eyes that locked on mine and made passionate promises.

"Come back to my dressing room. Maybe I can help you."

Zach's muttonchops threatened to catch fire, but the lady was in control. He stepped aside and we followed her to the dressing room, my heart pounding as her well-shaped derriere swayed before me. I had heard stories about actresses.

She shut the door behind us.

"It seems like a good crowd you have out there," I said, to prevent my tongue from sticking to the roof of my mouth. The large, cluttered room smelled of greasepaint and womanly scents. TR was staring with fascination at the makeup, props, and lighting equipment scattered about.

"Let me see the picture."

I handed it to her. She flinched.

"You know her," I stated.

"Maybe," she said, stepping in close. "I know a cock-and-bull story when I hear one—been around bad actors too long." Her hand was toying with my collar. She leaned against me, closed her eyes, and pressed her lips to mine. Her lips were surprisingly cold. Or maybe it was just that I was dizzingly warm. I opened my eyes and saw a shocked TR staring at me.

"You just met her!" he said.

She gave him the patronizing smile women have used to put men in their place since Adam first said no to the apple.

"Why do you want to know about Millicent?" she asked me.

"Millicent?"

"You do not know your sister's name?" she asked sarcastically.

"Well, uh, I always thought of her as Milly."

"I see. What's your name?"

"Smith."

"John?"

"Actually, it's Jim."

"Hey, Rube!" she shouted suddenly.

Fortunately for TR and me, I had worked in a few carnivals during my travels across the country and knew what that shout meant. As the giant Zach burst through the door, I heisted a powder puff from the lady's dressing table and hit him in the face with it. He sneezed and rubbed his eyes. I struck him two fair blows in the stomach, and one low blow, which did far more good.

Roosevelt, meanwhile, had his hands full with a shorter man whose thick, muscular arms were covered with tattoos. Soon the man with the tattoos had joined the giant on the floor. I got my derringer out and covered them.

"Now we can resume our conversation," TR said. "What is your name?"

"Grace."

TR tried questioning her, but he was too much of a gentlemen to get anything more than her name and a lot of obscenities. I asked him if I could handle it. Curious to learn my techniques, he stepped aside.

"Grace, either you tell me what you know of the woman in the photo, or I will break Zach's fingers, one by one," I said levelly. "I've done it many times and I can tell you it's not a pretty sight or sound."

"You wouldn't dare," she said.

Zach struggled to rise. He gave up after I kicked him in the belly. I handed my gun to TR. As Zach lay on the ground, I took his left hand, twisting his arm so he let out a yelp. Grace watched without any show of concern.

The tattooed man was frozen in place. Out of the corner of my eye I saw TR trying to control his disgust. I took Zach's fingers and spread them apart. I had my meanest scowl on my face.

Grace admired her nails.

"Tell him, tell him," Zach bellowed.

"Shut up," she ordered.

I wondered how long I could continue my bluff before I'd actually have to twist Zach's fingers.

"Millicent Albert, that's her name," Zach said. "She lived over at the Hotel Clarendon with a man she wasn't married to."

"Shut up," Grace said.

"You must cease immediately," the president told me.

I let up on the pressure. "Why is Grace so protective of Millicent? Who did Millicent hang around with?"

"Look out!" TR yelled.

I spun and ducked, sidestepping the six-inch hatpin Grace had tried to bury in my neck. To avoid becoming a pincushion, I had let go of Zach. He jumped up, his teeth bared, his fists balled.

"You sniveling coward," she sneered at him, holding the hatpin like a knife aimed at my heart.

"It's easy for you to talk, it wasn't your finger," he said, his barrel chest heaving as he made ready to charge.

"Wait until I tell Spike," she said.

It put him over the edge. He rushed me like a mad bull. I dodged and thwacked him with a wooden chair. The chair broke, but his spirit didn't. He got set to charge again.

"I will shoot if I have to," TR said, and the giant could see that he meant it. I scooped up the picture.

"Get him, get him," Grace shouted.

They moved slowly toward us as we backed to the door. We continued our little dance out into the corridor. We could hear actors going through their melodramatic performance on the nearby stage.

We backpedaled down the hall to the exit, with Grace urging Zach to attack. Bit players and stagehands surrounded us. They saw TR's steady finger on the trigger of the gun and decided to sit the ruckus out.

We reached the street, where they hurled curses at us, but nothing more damaging. We walked a good distance and I pocketed the gun.

"I wouldn't have broken his finger," I said when I saw the president studying me strangely.

He was silent as we walked.

"We're on a hot trail," I said. "It's like bear hunting. When you see warm scat it means you're getting near the beast. The reception we just got was steaming."

I admit it, I was feeling cocksure. I should have known better, but I thought we would soon see the whole matter wrapped up in a neat bundle.

The Hotel Clarendon was a shabby four-story clapboard structure that looked out on the depot of the Union Ferry Company—the Gateway to Brooklyn—at Furman and Fulton Streets. Located in the shadow of the Brooklyn Bridge, it was home to seafaring men and those who worked on the docks. Margaret Anders or Millicent or Minnie or whatever her name was must have been one tough customer to live there.

The lobby of the hotel was bare but for two chairs. In one, an elderly man with a beard that reached the rope holding his pants up, dozed unawares. He rested his feet on the other chair. His soles needed repair. So did the chairs. A grandfather clock ticked in a corner. It was two hours off. A sign warned, "No spitting or cussing—the management."

The desk clerk had a neatly waxed mustache and thinning hair on top of his head, which he kept patting down. He gave me a cagey look after a gander at the picture of the mystery woman.

"She is quite a looker," he said with a wink. "But I know one who makes her look like a boy. This is a colored girl, but I can tell you gents—"

"You disgusting ponce, I ought to give you a sound thrashing," TR blurted before I could shush him. "Do we look like the sort of men who would consort with trollops?"

The clerk patted his hair. "Yup."

Before TR made good on his threat, I made peace with the story about our beloved sister. I began idly tossing a gold piece in the air.

"What name did she sign in under?"

"She used the name Marla Aguilar. I don't have time to check into the identities of our guests."

"I am sure business would drop off rapidly if you did," TR piped up angrily. "What about her boyfriend?"

"You mean he was not her husband?"

"Let's not play games," I said.

He stared at the coin. The only sound was the ticking of the clock. I flipped the coin to him.

"He called himself Raoul Aguilar most of the time. A Spanish gentleman. Told me he had a coffee plantation in South America. He stayed here a month or so after she left. Quite distraught. Then I heard he got in trouble. Last I heard he was in jail."

"Let us see his room?"

He checked the board behind him. "There's no one in it—Three C."

Behind the flimsy door to 3C was a room as depressing as the worst fleabag I ever stayed in. The mirror on the bureau was cracked, the gas lamps sooty; the bed looked like a Barnum elephant had slept in it; the window faced a brick wall a foot away. We went over the room carefully but found no clues.

The outside of the twenty-five-year-old Raymond Street Jail resembled a castle; the inside looked like a dungeon. The gray granite-block building made strong men weak, and weak men mean.

Two bulls brought Aguilar out. They were both over six feet and had a quarter ton between them. He was little more than five feet, and probably a hundred pounds soaking wet. The striped prisoner's uniform he wore hung from his frame like a wash from a clothesline. His mustache was as limp as his body when the guards dumped him onto a wooden stool and chained his handcuffs to a screw eye in the wall. He had a sad expression on his face.

"Five minutes," a bull bellowed, and swaggered away.

"Raoul, my name is Moose," TR said. "This is my associate, Jim. We want to talk to you about Marla."

He looked even sadder. "What is there to say? She is dead. I am in jail. She was a real money maker. It hurt me so when she left."

We waited, but he sat looking off until TR coaxed him by saying, "What happened?"

Suddenly, he looked like a cornered rat instead of a sad bunny. "Why are you asking all these questions? Why do you want to know about Marla?" he asked.

"We are looking into her murder."

"For who?"

"She became friendly with a gentleman who is very upset about her death. He hired me to see what I could learn. The police have neither the resources nor the inclination to probe very deeply."

"Marla was a whore," he hissed. "I taught her everything she knew. At her first chance, she ran off."

"Who did she run off with?"

"The police were by. I didn't tell them anything. Why should I tell you?"

"It was coppers who put you in here," I said. "We had nothing to do with it. We don't even know why you're here."

"Because of the man she went away with. He had me framed. I was charged with stabbing a drunk in a bar. I was not even in that part of the city when it happened. But this man, he can get as many lying witnesses as he wants."

Aguilar had the convict's knack of talking without moving his lips so the guards couldn't spot it. I reckoned this was not his first time in prison.

"That's terrible," TR said sincerely. "Perhaps if you told us the name of the man who stole your lady friend, we would be able to see him brought to justice."

Aguilar laughed.

"Rest assured my client is a powerful man who can cause whoever stole Marla a fair amount of grief," TR said.

"Who is your client?"

"That is confidential," TR said. "But he carries a lot of weight. He might be able to help you."

"I don't need anybody's help," Aguilar said. The prisoner was boasting and we all knew it, all the more ridiculous because he sat chained to the wall like an animal. We waited. He looked both ways and said, "Spike. He took her."

"What is his full name? Where do we find him?" TR asked.

"I do not know him by any other name, or where he lives or works. He always found me."

"At the hotel?" TR asked.

"Yes. And before that, when we lived on Ninth Street, by the Gowanus Canal. He is able to find whoever he wants, whenever he wants to."

"What does he look like?" TR asked.

"Average height, average weight. Dark hair, dark eyes."

"I think I know the man," I said sarcastically.

"He is an educated man, very well dressed, sounds almost British."

"Anything else?" TR was fidgeting with excitement. "Does he walk with a limp, smoke a certain brand of cigarettes, have any scars, spectacles, tattoos?"

"No scars or tattoos or glasses. He is a gentleman like myself. At least he was. Recently, he has changed, begun acting like a madman at times. I have heard that he——"

A bull had been sidling closer. "Time's up," he said, and, without waiting, undid Aguilar's chain and gave him a jerk. Aguilar did not look back as he was led off.

"We should try Aguilar's old neighborhood," I suggested. "Red Hook is a crowded area. You never know what a neighbor might have seen. Maybe you could go back to Sagamore Hill and I'll go see what's up."

TR would have none of that.

"Won't they miss you at Sagamore?" I tried, as we hopped aboard a southbound streetcar.

"They are used to my disappearing. Usually it means I have gone off riding or camping. It puts Marlowe in a tizzy."

"Marlowe?"

"The head of the Secret Service detail at Sagamore. He is concerned that if I am killed, it will ruin his possibilities for advancement."

"I reckon it would."

"Maybe. Or maybe it would guarantee it."

Red Hook was home to a passel of immigrants. The sounds of Irish, Italian, and Jewish voices—mostly mothers hanging from windows and yelling to their young 'uns—filled the air. No matter what the nationalities, the children ignored the women.

The Gowanus Canal, a hundred-foot-wide channel with about a mile of waterway, shimmered nearby. Tugs from the Gowanus Towing Company tooted their whistles. Rich men's yachts on the way to the Twenty-third-Street Basin knifed through the dark green waters.

A half dozen young boys were spinning tops at the intersection nearest where Aguilar had said he had lived. Their clothes were worn but clean. An older boy, about fourteen, played with them, even though he was missing most of the fingers on his right hand. He had a freckled face and a cap that rested on big ears.

"Do any of you know Raoul Aguilar?" TR asked.

The boys looked up and shook their heads. "Maybe," the older kid said. "Who wants to know?"

"Someone he owes money to."

"You ain't coppers?"

"No."

"How much does he owe?"

"A hundred dollars."

The younger boys whistled.

"What would you pay to find him?"

"Let's walk and talk," Mr. Roosevelt suggested.

Away from the others, the skinny lad dropped the hard-nosed act. The cap kept flopping down into his face.

"We know Aguilar is in jail," TR said. "I am more interested in finding out his background. Who his friends were, that sort of thing."

"No one from around here. He had lotsa fellas used to come around. Clumbians, at least that's what I heard. They were speaking Spanish. The way they was talking, it sounded like Italian, but Juan said they were Clumbians."

"Clumbians?" I asked.

"Yeah. Juan, he's from Cuba and he says they speak one kind of Spanish there, and another kind in Clumbia."

He saw me glancing at his fingers.

"I used to have a good job in a mill in South Brooklyn," the youth said. "A dollar a day, six days a week. There's people that would kill for a job like that. I was sleepy at work one day. Sleepy and sloppy. I was lucky they stopped the machine before it bit off the whole hand."

He said it very smoothly, a story he had told many times.

"I can pick up a few bits now and then begging, but I'm only missing a little. There's one at the park, younger than me and missing both arms. Competition is tough."

"The men who came for Aguilar, how were they dressed?" I asked.

"Like swells. Monkey suits, top hats. They make good targets," he said, mimicking throwing a snowball.

The president described Spike and asked if he had ever been seen. The youngster said no. After a few more questions, but no valuable answers, TR rewarded him with a gold eagle.

"Thanks," he said, and took off before we could change our minds.

We made a few more stops, but didn't learn much about Aguilar or his woman. We met poor but honest folk living in cramped apartments.

"It is too easy to forget how it is," TR said, after our final fruitless march to the top of a four-story walk-up.

"Not if you live here," I said.

"Not if you live here," he echoed.

five

We had learned all we could in the borough of Kings and the president suggested we mosey over to Manhattan to see Arthur Brown, a *New York World* reporter he knew from his days as police commissioner.

TR wanted to walk across the Brooklyn Bridge, to kick theories around in his noodle and enjoy the view of the growing city on both sides of the East River.

We reached mid-bridge and rested for a few minutes, watching the sun setting over the New Jersey shore. It was a peculiar feeling, living on the edge of America.

"What a great city," TR said, as he came out of his brief funk. "What a great nation. Much has been given us and much will rightfully be expected from us."

We passed above the Fulton Fish Market, which smelled worse than a cowboy after a month on the trail, then headed over to Newspaper Row. The buildings housing the *New York World, Sun, Tribune, Times,* and *Evening Post* towered over City Hall. Grandest of them all was the eleven-story, gold-domed Pulitzer building, where Brown labored over tomorrow's fish wrapping.

TR told me Brown's many years in the business had gotten him a desk near the window in the stuffy, overcrowded, and hectic city room. When not at his desk, he was at the press shack opposite police headquarters on Mulberry Street, or roving the alleyways of the city.

Brown, a stoop-shouldered man with white hair and a broken-blood-vesseled nose, sat clickety-clacking away on his typewriting gadget. He was wearing a vest that didn't match his pants, and a white shirt that looked like it had been used to blot up coffee.

"What can I do you for?" Brown asked, quickly glancing up and then returning his attention to his writing.

"Do not say anything, Brownie, but it's your old buddy from the police commission," the president whispered.

Brown did a double-take. "Holy Jesus," he said.

The newsmen working at neighboring desks looked up, saw we were neither bathing beauties, celebrities, nor likely subjects for a scoop, and ignored us.

"What's going on?" Brown asked, lighting a cigarette.

"This is Jim White. A friend. We need your help."

"Boy!" Brown yelled, ripping the sheet from his typewriter. An eager young man with dark hair and pale skin galloped over. "Get this to Smitty and tell him if he doesn't give me four columns on page one, I will let the anarchists know where he lives. I'll be back to finish it later."

The copyboy nodded seriously, took the paper, and hurried off. Brown got a straw skimmer from a hat rack and signaled for us to follow. The newsman was laughing loudly by the time we reached the street.

"What a tale, what a tale," he said. "The president of the United States appears in the newsroom of a major metropolitan daily, and no one recognizes him. Mark Twain could not write something so funny."

"But you must tell no one," I cautioned.

"Don't worry," Mr. Roosevelt said. "I know Brownie. He is as good at keeping secrets as he is at spreading the truth."

"Thank you, Teddy—I mean, Mr. President."

He led us to The Wharf Rat, an ale house on Catherine Slip near the East River. We had to walk that far from Newspaper Row to find a bar not crawling with reporters.

"I must have your word that my appearance and everything I say will be kept absolutely confidential," TR said, when we settled into a rear booth.

"Is it that important?" Brown asked.

"Indeed it is."

Brown removed his skimmer and put his hand over his heart. "You have my word."

"Bully. Have you heard the name Spike?"

Brown took a gulp of the Scotch whisky the barkeep set before him. He tried to keep a casual look, but I could hear his reporter's clockwork ticking.

"It's a problem I have," I said, hoping to bamboozle him.

Brown gave me a scornful look. "Hah! The president just happens to tag along to carry your coat? It is obviously something involving Mr. Roosevelt, so don't try and pull the wool over my eyes."

TR smiled at me. "You should know better than to lie to a newspaperman. They invented the trick." TR paused and twiddled his mustache. "Brownie here has caught more dishonest politicians with his pen than anyone I know." Brown relaxed under TR's diplomatic combination of jest and flattery. I decided to keep quiet.

"The man you are talking about is extremely dangerous," Brown said, as more Scotch disappeared down his gullet. "He has ties to the Black Hand, to Five Corners plug-uglies, to hoodlums and gangsters up and down the coast, and as far west as California."

"What else do you know about him?" TR asked.

"Painfully little. One of our reporters started sniffing around a few years back. He was scared off or bought off or both. We never even nailed down Spike's true name. Last I heard he had moved up in the world, but it's all vague. For example, someone might boast of working for Spike to get out of a pinch. Whether they actually are, or are just using his name, is open to conjecture."

"Have you ever heard of him in connection with a theater in Brooklyn called the Grand Opera House? Or a massive brute named Zach, another ruffian with tattoos, and a woman named Grace? There is also a ponce named Raoul Aguilar and a woman who went by the name Marla Aguilar, Millicent Albert, Minnie Adams."

"Well, you will have to buy me at least another drink if you want me to check into all that."

A reasonable price. TR paid it, and then paid it again. I suspected Brown was trying to get us drunk, to find out what we were up to. But I could down brew with the best of them and TR nursed one drink for our three. By the sixth round, Brown and I were friends, and leaning on each other for support.

"It is a grand time we live in," Brown said. "Do you realize that one out of fifty people in these forty-five states now has a telephone? The average American—if there can be said to be such a thing—earns a quarter an hour. A spanking new automobile costs fifteen hundred dollars. If you cannot afford one, there are over a million miles of trolley track. Most important of all, better than two thousand newshpapers. With fifteen million readers." He belched.

"God bless America," I said.

"And we have the best damn president in the Executive Mansion shince Abraham Lincoln."

"Thank you," TR said, looking uncomfortable with the drunken praise. "I prefer to call it the White House. Executive Mansion sounds too stuffy. You should see Quentin on stilts, or Archie on roller skates, or even dear sweet Alice sliding down the banister. It does not look very executive then."

"I would like to shee that."

"You are invited. We shall be going to Washington shortly. If you garner any information, come down and deliver it personally."

The drunken newsman was clearly thrilled. TR had played him exactly right. "Lishen, Teddy, I know you are a tough cuss, but be careful. Shpike has lots of friends and most of them would jusht as soon kill you as look at you." Brown staggered out of the bar to complete his column.

We had a long trip ahead of us back to Oyster Bay. The thought of hitting the hay was mighty appealing. Mr. Roosevelt, though seven years older than me, was rarin' for more excitement. Unfortunately, he got what he wanted.

It was dark and deserted down by the waterfront. Most of the gaslights were broken. Water lapped against the wooden pilings. Horses in the distance clopped down cobblestones. TR always did have ears that were more sensitive than most folks, and I had a lot of liquor sloshing around in me, so the first I knew we were in trouble was when I saw him stiffen.

"What's going on?" I asked, reaching under my vest and gripping the derringer. I wished I was more sober.

"There are two men following us," TR said.

As I turned, three more jumped out of a doorway in front of us. I drew my gun, but before I could aim, they swung billy clubs.

"Oh, you want to put up a fight?" sneered a man with a tiny head mounted on a huge body. He had a dirty blond beard and cruel eyes.

My arm went numb as he smashed his club into it. The derringer clattered to the pavement. Another thug swung at the president. Our two pursuers joined the attack. They shoved us over near the water, behind a pile of cargo, out of sight of even the occasional passerby.

"Why are you asking questions?" demanded the lead villain, who had a nose that had been broken more times than a Tammany politician's word.

"It is none of your business," TR responded.

"Our sister's disappeared," I said.

"Marla did not have any brothers," Broken Nose said, and struck me. "You tried that sucker game with Grace."

They used fists, clubs, and boots on us. The last thing I saw before losing consciousness was TR getting in a good punch on the lead villain, and taking two in return from his accomplices. His glasses went flying.

I awoke to the poke of a stick in my side. I tried to push it away.

"Oh, a bit of life is coming back to ya," a voice said with a brogue as thick as mulligan stew.

It wasn't easy opening my eyes. A nearby gas lamp made a small pool of light in the pitch-black night. A well-fed patrolman was standing over me, prodding me not too gently with his nightstick. I looked over to see TR sprawled on the ground. I scrambled to him.

"Quick, this man is the president of the United States. We must get him to a hospital."

The copper laughed. "I have heard of seeing pink elephants but never drunken presidents. You boyos have too much to drink?"

TR groaned.

"Ah, Mr. President, the problems of running the country must weigh heavily on you," the copper said.

TR sat up. He had a thin trickle of blood running from his forehead and the side of his face was bruised. His clothes were torn. He felt around on the pavement until he touched his glasses. He put them on. One lens was cracked.

"Sure'n you do look like a gentleman," the copper said. He gave me a thwack with the stick. "Now get up and be on your way or I'll call the Black Maria."

"But this man is—"

"Sorry for getting drunk," TR interrupted. "My companion and

I will leave immediately, officer." He struggled to his feet. "Come, come, Jim. We must swear off John Barleycorn." He wobbled as he bent to fetch the derby he had been lying on. He tried to block it back into shape. The patrolman made clucking noises as we stumbled down the street.

"How are you feeling?" he asked, as soon as we were out of earshot.

"Like a horse rolled over me. But what about you? I think we should get you to a hospital."

"I've had worse injuries. We cannot risk my being identified. You must remember, at all costs, no one must know who I am."

"But what if—"

"No what ifs. I accept the risks. If a man has the right stuff in him, his will grows stronger and stronger with each exercise of it—and if he doesn't have the right stuff he had better keep clear of dangerous game-hunting or anything else in which there is bodily peril."

As our train pulled into Jamaica Station, an elderly woman with the snooty air of royalty prepared to sit near us, saw our condition, sniffed disgustedly, and moved off. TR burst into such jolly laughter I could not help but join him.

"It is really not as bad as it looks," TR said. "My padding absorbed much of the fury of their blows. The only problem is, the vision in my left eye is blurred."

"The lens is cracked."

"It's not that. But I am sure it will pass."

"What'll we tell the staff when we get in?"

"We need not say anything. They are quite used to me coming back from my adventures a trifle scuffed."

Our horse and carriage were safely stored in a barn near the train station in Oyster Bay.

Mr. Roosevelt used water from the pump to wash the dried blood from his face and the oil from his hair. A little solvent took the mustache wax right out. I also cleaned up at the pump.

"I never liked this hat anyway," he said, cutting holes in the derby and setting it atop the head of one of the mules. "It looks better on him than me."

When the mule gnawed the brim, he took it away and tossed it into the garbage. He took the padding from around his middle, folded it, and hid it under a pile of hay. From a wooden box in the buckboard he fetched a spare set of spectacles.

"Your vision, how is it?" I asked.

He shrugged. "I'm quite sure it will be better in the morning."

We climbed on the buckboard, I cracked the whip, and we made good time down the winding dirt roads.

The house at Sagamore Hill was brightly lit as we approached. The guard at the gate leveled a shotgun at us, until he realized who we were. He saluted and waved us through.

A stable hand came out and took care of the carriage. He noticed our banged-up condition but didn't say anything.

We entered the house and Audrey McFarlane hurried over. She stared at TR, and then me. "Mr. Roosevelt," she whispered. "You ought to know—"

"Come, come, dear, no need to whisper," the president said as he peeled off his two-sizes-too-big coat in the entrance hall.

But we quickly saw why she spoke softly.

From out of the drawing room came Edith Kermit Carow Roosevelt.

SIX

Mrs. Roosevelt had the kind of long nose and soft skin that a painter would love. Her mouth was wide, her jaw firm. She was forty-one years old and wasn't ashamed of it. She was not the kind rowdies would whistle at, but she could turn heads. It was how she carried herself, thoroughbred all the way.

"Hello, Theodore," she said in a voice as cultured as her appearance. I could understand why Mr. Roosevelt believed women to be the equals of men. Looking at this regal lady in pleated chiffon and lace, I wondered if they were our superiors.

"Uh, hello, dear," he said.

There was a long awkward silence, which the maid used to slip away. I wanted to join her, for more reasons than one.

"Do you intend to introduce your friend to me or must I make introductions myself?"

"Of course, of course. This is Jim White, an old chum from the Badlands and the First Cavalry."

I felt I should bow and kiss her hand. Instead, I said, "We have met before, though I doubt that you would remember, ma'am."

"But I do. When the Rough Riders were mustered out."

"I am mighty flattered."

"Theodore spoke very highly of you then. What mischief have you two gotten into?"

I didn't know what the president wanted to tell her, so I hemmed and hawed.

"Mr. White, you are welcome as a guest in my home, as long as you promise not to get Mr. Roosevelt killed," she said, taking a few steps toward the drawing room. "Theodore, if I might have a word with you."

He followed her and took a seat on the button-back sofa. She sat at a small white writing desk and shook her head. He looked like a schoolboy about to get a lickin' after dipping a girl's pigtail in an inkwell.

I went quietly up the stairs. As I was about to enter my bedroom, I saw the door to the southeast bedroom, which had been open a crack, close suddenly. I knew the maid's room was on the floor above and wondered who the room belonged to.

A pair of pajamas was hanging in the closet. I put them on. They made me feel like a real gentleman, since my nighttime attire was either long johns or my birthday suit. I set my head on the down pillow and looked at the ceiling, unable to sleep after the day's excitement. I lit the gas lamp and paced around, admiring the illustrations on the wall. They were from TR's book, *Hunting Trips of a Ranchman*. I was thinking about going down to the library to borrow a book when there was a quick knock at the door. Could it be McFarlane come to answer my fantasies?

"Come in," I said eagerly.

Wearing a long pink nightdress—her hair a tangled brown bird's nest held together with a half-dozen pins—Alice Lee Roosevelt walked into my room.

"What are you doing here?" I demanded, uncomfortable standing in my pajamas before the president's seventeen-year-old daughter.

She put a slender finger to her pouty lips. "Shhhhh. They're still awake."

The teenage "Princess Alice" had as much of a knack as her father for getting into the paper. She went swimming in a pool fully clothed, and pulled two members of the diplomatic corps in after her; she had been known to keep a garter snake in her purse; she traveled widely and, like her father, was never afraid to speak her mind. She was a peculiar mixture of girl and woman. With her perfectly sculpted head at a slight tilt, she studied me with cool blue eyes.

"What have you and my father been up to?" she asked in a hushed voice.

"What are you doing here?" I repeated.

"Trying to find out what is going on, silly."

"A lady does not come into a gentleman's bedroom," I said sternly.

She giggled. "How did you get that shiner?"

I looked in the mirror. My eye was puffy, getting black and blue. "Go to your bedroom at once."

"I could scream for help and tell everyone you dragged me in here to steal me away and sell to white-slavers." She opened her mouth wide as if to holler.

"I wouldn't do such a rotten thing to any white-slaver I know."

It took a second for what I had said to sink in. She smiled. "Do you really know white-slavers?"

I nodded. In truth, I knew some men who I had suspicions about.

"Tell me about them. What are they like? Do they really drug girls who go to nickelodeons alone and sell them to Chinamen? Is it true there are opium dens with women chained to the wall?"

"This is hardly conversation for a young lady, let alone a thing to discuss before bedtime. It will give you bad dreams."

"I never have bad dreams," she said. "I heard the maid say you were a cowboy. Did you ever bust a bronco? Or shoot an Indian? Did you ever see anyone scalped? Is it true Papa was a great cowboy? Do animals go crazy from locoweed? Are there poisoned water holes with dead animals piled up next to them?"

I took a couple of steps toward her. She stood defiant and unafraid. I took her right arm firmly and herded her to the door. "Your father was a rootin' tootin' cowboy. As for the other questions, you're gonna have to wait until tomorrow."

I opened the door. She turned suddenly, gave me a peck on the cheek, and scurried down the hall to her room.

My big mistake was not locking the bedroom door.

"One move and we scalp ya," a small voice said. Two Indians with warpainted faces and crude tomahawks were glaring at me.

For a fraction of a second, I thought I was in a nightmare. Unlike Alice, I did have bad dreams, of death and suffering I'd seen on the plains and in the cities. But the faces of the Indians looking down on me were more cherubic than savage.

"Are you Archie?" I asked the larger, ten-year-old with a mass of blond hair, big eyes, and blue overalls.

"Awwh, he knew," the smaller one said, a boy of six with shorter-cut hair and an impish expression.

"And you must be Quentin," I said to him.

"Chief Quenty-Quee of the Roosevelt tribe."

"I am Chief Sagamore Mohanis," Archie said.

They whooped and wriggled as I lifted both of them, put one under either arm, and took them to the door.

"I'll see you later," I said as I released them.

Archie, lifted his tomahawk over Quentin's head. "Lizzie Borden took an ax and gave her mother forty whacks."

Quentin yelled as Archie swung and they raced the length of the hall. I could hear the rhyme continue as they scampered down the stairs. "When she saw what she had done, she gave her father forty-one." Although they were barefoot, they sounded like a fast-moving army.

I was sore down to my very bones and had black-and-blue marks all over my body. My face felt tender as I shaved.

Dressed and ready to face the day, I wandered downstairs. TR and Mrs. R were heading out, carrying a wicker picnic basket.

"I will be with you momentarily," TR said to his missus. She nodded, and went to sit in her front room. TR gestured me into his study.

"I promised to take Edie rowing," he said softly. "We can get back to work later today." He was off, and I went to the kitchen. My belly was grumbling something fierce.

Annie O'Rourke offered me a piece of steak to put on my shiner, but I declined. I sat at the sturdy kitchen table as she made me a breakfast of hot biscuits and gravy. She was baking bread and the room was filled with intoxicatingly homey odors.

"Where is Audrey McFarlane?" I asked casually.

"She's a fine one, isn't she?" O'Rourke said with a maternal wink.

"Uh, yes, she seems to be quite a nice young lady."

"She is. Today is her day off."

"Do you know where I could find her?" I asked, throwing caution to the winds.

"I saw her go walking near Oyster Bay Harbor. It was not that long ago. You still might catch her."

I grabbed a last biscuit, thanked O'Rourke, and hurried out. From the other side of the ice house, I heard war whoops. Archie and Quentin had climbed the tower of the windmill-water pump and were shouting with all the strength in their little lungs.

"Come join us," Quentin said. I waved and hurried on.

"Where's the hurry, mate?" a Secret Serviceman asked as I barreled down the grassy hillside. He had a spyglass in his hand and a pistol tucked in his belt. He was tall, broad-shouldered, with a derby riding atop his head. He had a friendly manner and you could tell he did well with the ladies.

"May I borrow that?" I asked, pointing to his telescope.

He handed it to me. "The president and her ladyship are on the water."

"Ow," I said, accidentally putting the spyglass to my bruised eye.

"Quite a shiner," he commented. "How did you come by it?"

I sighted Mr. and Mrs. Roosevelt in a rowboat. He was working the oars while she read to him from a book. I moved the glass around the shore and spotted Audrey.

"I said, how did you come by it?" the Secret Serviceman repeated.

"It's a long story. I was clumsy."

"It looks like a souvenir of a fight. I saw you were moving a might stiffly. Did you and the president get into a brouhaha when you snuck away?"

I turned to him. "What do you mean, snuck away?"

"We try to tag along behind the president on his forays, but you managed to evade us yesterday. Marlowe has us periodically check the barns in town, finding out who is hiding wagons for Mr. Roosevelt. But we never can keep up. Where did you go?"

"What is your name?"

"William Heinz."

"Jim White," I said, and we shook hands. "I better be on my way. It was a pleasure meeting you."

I returned his glass and took off toward where Audrey sat on a blanket. I moved quickly, though wary of the occasional patches of poison ivy and bramble bushes. When I neared her, I slowed down to a saunter, put my hands in my pockets, and began whistling "Queen of the Bicycle Girls."

"Oh, I hope I didn't disturb you," I said as I pretended to pass near her accidentally.

She smiled. Next to her lay a copy of the *Ladies' Home Journal,* the cover showing a fop with his arms around a lady in a silk gown. She saw me glancing at the magazine and blushed nearly as red as the cover.

"There are lots of interesting articles about being handy in the household," she said.

"I must confess, it's not on my regular reading list."

She laughed. "What do you read, *Nick Carter?*"

"Yes. And Twain, Browning, Wordsworth, Poe, the Sunday funnies."

"I love Browning," she gushed. "Did you know Mr. and Mrs. Roosevelt met him on their honeymoon? They read his works to each other all the time."

"The year's at the spring; And day's at the morn; Mornings at seven; The hillside's dew-pearled," I returned.

"The lark's on the wing; the snail's on the thorn; God's in his heaven—All's right with the world," she responded. "I would never have figured you for a man who knew poetry."

"I can thank Mr. Roosevelt for that," I told her. It was a perfect way to launch into our adventures in the Badlands. Maybe I stretched the truth a smidgen, but I don't think she minded.

We wound up rowing from Oyster Bay Harbor to Cold Spring Harbor, and then back again. The president and his missus gave us friendly waves when we passed. We saw rich boys from the Seawanhaka Yacht Club and numerous waterfowl. McFarlane had enough in her picnic basket for two, which made me wonder how much of a coincidence my finding her was.

She was a fascinating colleen. Her father had been a farrier in

County Cork. He came to the United States in 1844, during the Great Potato Famine. Audrey Maureen McFarlane had been born on Bloomingdale Road in a squatter's hovel in the western area of what is now Central Park. Their area was called Shanty Town. Only the poorest Irish and Negroes lived there.

Her father was as ambitious as he was lucky. He made enough money to move them to Harlem. He pushed her to get an education. Audrey married a shopkeeper, who died of diphtheria after a year of marriage. She had gone West as a Fred Harvey girl, and we talked about how our paths might have crossed.

Audrey told me about the smooth-talkers who made her propositions and my green-eyed monster stirred. I turned the conversation toward how McFarlane and the rest of the help felt about the president and his family.

While the children were considered handfuls, they were loved by the staff, who had all been with the Roosevelts for years. Audrey made it sound like the servants—which included herself, O'Rourke, Molly the seamstress, Miss Young, the children's tutor, as well as a groundskeeper, coachman, stable hand, and gardener—were treated like family.

By the time we got back to shore, it was mid-afternoon.

"You're a strange one, James White. Sometimes you sound like an unsophisticated cowhand. Other times, I get the feeling you know a lot more than you let on."

"Shucks, ma'am," I said, grinding my toe into the dirt.

She rewarded me with her musical laugh and a light kiss. We strolled up from the water. She let go of my hand as the house came into view.

"I hope we do this again," I said. "It was dee-lightful."

She giggled at my imitation of our boss. "I hope so too," she said, before running into the house ahead of me. I hung back, leaning against a copper beech that looked like the foot of a gargantuan circus elephant. When I felt enough time had passed, I entered.

From the library I could hear TR and the harsh voice of another man. I walked past, glancing in from the corner of my eye. The visitor sat in a chair facing TR's desk. He was huge, with thick devilish eyebrows over deep-set eyes. An expensive, dark suit covered his large figure.

TR saw me, but made no acknowledgment. He pounded the desktop with a meaty fist. A riled-up president, let alone a leader as dynamic as Theodore Roosevelt, would have scared the pants off of most men. But not the muckety-muck facing TR now.

The man, known as "Jupiter" for both his size and influence, was shouting, angrily gesturing with thick fingers. It was an impressive and frightening battle between titans. For the man flapping his jaws at TR was none other than the king of the robber barons, John Pierpont Morgan.

seven

I couldn't make out many of their words, but I did hear "confrontation . . . threat . . . shall not be intimidated" from TR, and "does not frighten me . . . go ahead and try" from Morgan.

Jupiter got up and slammed the door in my face. It was probably one of the only times in his life that he opened or shut a door for himself.

Unlike most of the other robber barons, the sixty-five-year-old Morgan had been born with a silver spoon in his mouth. When his father died, he left J.P. ten million dollars. That could pay the rent for a few years!

Morgan, through his banking interests and savvy financial maneuvers, was the most powerful robber baron. The process of big railroad companies gobbling up smaller ones had come to be called "Morganization." Not much had been written about Morgan because he disliked publicity and had the muscle to make sure he did not get much. But TR had told me quite a bit.

As a young man, Jupiter had been involved in the sale of defective guns to the Union Army, as well as gold speculation at our country's expense. His feuds with fellow robber barons Jay Gould and James Fisk over the control of the Albany and Susquehanna

Railroads were the stuff of legends. Besides court battles where judges were bought and sold, armies of plug-uglies ripped up rails and fought with fists and clubs for control. Morgan had won, of course. There weren't many struggles he had lost.

The same could certainly be said of Theodore Roosevelt.

I lingered in the entrance hall, hoping I could hear what was going on. It was like trying to guess the outcome of the Jack Johnson—Jim Jeffries match by listening through the canvas. I walked further into the house and spotted Audrey and Molly, the seamstress, chattering.

"How long has Mr. Roosevelt had company?" I asked.

"They've been going at it for close to an hour," Molly answered. "I hope they don't come to blows."

"If they do, I wager on Mr. Roosevelt, even though Morgan has got the reach."

The women did not find it funny. Molly gave me an annoyed look and went upstairs.

"Would you like to hear what they are saying?" Audrey asked in a hushed voice.

"I tried."

"Come with me," she said with a wink, and we went to the basement door. She looked to see that no one was watching and opened it. She took a candle from a small inset shelf and we made our way downstairs.

There was nothing remarkable about the musty-smelling cellar. It contained a few trunks that couldn't fit in the trunk room upstairs, cords of firewood, and a few extra chairs. We walked to a spot underneath the library. I could hear the two men speak as clearly as if I were sitting on Mr. Roosevelt's lap. McFarlane indicated I should be silent and pointed to a vent leading to the room through which the sound was filtering.

I gave her a quick thank-you kiss and she stifled a giggle. I moved a chair over, removed the sheet that had been protecting it from the dust, and sat. McFarlane stood expectantly. I felt like I should shoo her away—the secret affairs of important men were not the business of womenfolk—but how could I chase the person who had put me in the catbird seat? I got her a chair. All the while, I had been listening to the men above us.

". . . Rockefeller, Frick, Carnegie, Crittenden, and yourself think this country can be bought and sold like a piece of property you choose to speculate in," TR was saying.

"You can keep the fiery rhetoric to yourself, Teddy. It does not impress me the way it does the unwashed hordes."

Despite its wide use in the popular press, I knew that Mr. Roosevelt did not like being called "Teddy," especially with the patronizing sound that Morgan put into it. I could imagine the color rising in TR's face.

"I secure the passage of a law, over the best efforts of your accomplices like Hanna or Aldrich, and you try and turn it against me," TR said. "I pushed through the railroad safety laws providing for improved airbrakes and the like. So you and your railroad magnate chums say you shall reduce wages and increase prices to make up for it, painting the government as the villain."

"Would our country be criss-crossed by railroads, would our factories be booming, if it were not for men with drive and vigor who fought for their vision?" Morgan bellowed.

"What are your selfish visionaries doing to this great nation as they greedily grab pieces of the pie? What do they plan to leave for our children, and our children's children?"

"Come, come now, Teddy, the waves of populism that Jennings Bryan fostered have ebbed. That sort of attitude is passé. This is the twentieth century. Our corporations will naturally control themselves by the laws of free enterprise in the marketplace."

"I am as much a supporter of free enterprise as any man alive," TR said. "However, monopolistic trusts serve no interests but their own. They crush the life blood out of an economy, a government, a people. You will bring about a corporate dictatorship if allowed to run unchecked."

The two men argued over the Sherman Antitrust Act of 1890, the 1895 Knight Company Supreme Court decision that TR said crippled the Act, and Attorney General Knox's filing of legal action against the Northern Securities Company to get the Act back on its feet. That action had brought Morgan out to Sagamore Hill from his estate further east on the north shore of Long Island.

The deal, as best I could understand it, involved the merger of E.H. Harriman's Union Pacific with northwestern routes controlled by James J. Hill and Ronald Crittenden. Morgan had arranged the deal, which got around the antitrust laws by using something called holding companies, where only shares of stock, not actual ownership, changed hands.

TR argued that the monopoly would lead to higher rates, price fixing, and discriminatory practices. Morgan said it would make for greater efficiency and actually save money for the railroads and ultimately the consumers.

"If we have done anything wrong, send your man to my man and we can fix it up," Jupiter said.

"What do you think I am, some rival operator who either intends to ruin your interests or else can be induced to make a mutually profitable peace?" TR said, biting every word. "It is not a matter of fixing it up, it is a matter of stopping an illegal act committed by people who can buy judges right up to the Supreme Court."

"What would Chief Justice Fuller say if he heard you speaking of the Court in such a manner?"

"You and your ilk think I am just another underpaid government official you can push around or ignore. The audacity, to send an emissary before my State of the Union address to tell me I should say nothing but platitudes. I have not forgiven that intrusion."

"It was merely a suggestion," Morgan said. "You have a tendency to be outspoken. I hoped you would not frighten the country by—"

"It is not the country that would be frightened. It is your pack of mendacious money-grubbers."

"Let us not degenerate into name calling," Morgan said. "If you're so concerned about the nation's health, go after the unions."

"Labor has as much right as capital to organize. It's tyranny to forbid this right, just as it is tyranny to misuse the power acquired by organization," TR said. "Whenever there's brutal indifference to the rights of others and shortsighted refusal to look beyond the moment's gain, then the offender, whether union or corporation, must be fought."

"So *that* will be the platform for your 1904 campaign?"

"I don't yet know whether I will run. There are many things that trouble me. I agreed to talk today because I wanted to send a message to you and your cronies. I want you all to know that I will not be intimidated in any way, legal or otherwise, from serving the American public."

"I don't understand what you're talking about?"

"Perhaps not. But I would appreciate it if you made your colleagues aware of my feelings."

"Have you thought of taking a vacation? Perhaps the affairs of state press too heavily on your shoulders," Morgan said sarcastically.

"I am as strong as a bull moose. Mark my words, Morgan, I can be just as ornery."

"Now listen, Teddy, you must not—"

"You listen to me. I want to destroy the evil in trusts, but not prosperity. If you and the others do not give the ordinary people a square deal, you will wake one morning to find tumbrels being wheeled to your mansions and guillotines being set up in the streets."

"You do have a flare for the dramatic," Morgan said.

"Our meeting is at an end, *Johnny*. I am expecting company."

"The German ambassador?"

"You are attuned to my affairs. Perhaps I should look more closely into yours."

I heard chairs scraping as the men got up. Their good-byes were colder than a creek in the Rockies after the spring thaw. I could hear the footfalls as the president walked Morgan to the door.

McFarlane did not have the puzzled look I expected to see on her pretty face.

"Mr. Roosevelt has quite a tough row to hoe," she said.

"You understood what went on?"

My sweet little maid launched into a recital of the president's economic policies, plans to punish discriminatory rebates in interstate commerce and expedite circuit-court action on antitrust cases. She explained holding companies, trusts, and mergers like a professor.

"But how do you know all that?"

"My father taught me."

"I thought he was just a blacksmith."

"That shows how much you know," she said haughtily. "A farrier is more of a veterinarian than a mere smithy. Besides, Mr. Roosevelt has been teaching me. He believes that women deserve the same opportunities as men, though I do not imagine you do."

"Oh no, I think women are defintely the equal of men. If not more so. But I thought all you would know how to do is manage a household budget. Why didn't you tell me?"

"You did not ask," she said with a smug smile.

I kissed her and apologized. She accepted. We were alone in the cellar. It was quiet and romantic. The candle was burning low, making a warm flickering light. I felt my passion growing as I held her pressed against me.

"I guess I talk too much," I said. "What else don't I know about you?"

"Men like to talk about themselves. Women prefer to keep their mystery."

I squeezed her fanny and let my hands roam. She broke away and took a few steps back. "Now, now, you cannot be solving my mysteries so easily."

I stepped toward her, and she hightailed it up the stairs, laughing. We came out of the basement. She turned back to me and brushed the dust from my sleeve.

"There, you look like a proper gentlemen."

"You are driving me mad, you little nymph."

With a toss of her hair and a smile, she disappeared into the kitchen.

Up in my room, I found a half dozen shirts, three pairs of pants, two pairs of shoes, and assorted haberdashery to completely outfit myself. There were two suits that had been perfectly tailored. There also was a brand-new derringer and a box of ammunition from Sears. The price was still on the gun—$6.25. It was a Remington, .41 caliber, rimfire, nickel-plated, with checkered rubber stock and a three-inch barrel.

I wanted to thank Mr. Roosevelt and find out where I could try out the weapon without jangling the nerves of his security staff. I changed outfits and hurried downstairs. Mrs. Roosevelt was in the drawing room. She summoned me. I sat before her nervously.

"I presume the clothing from Abercrombie and Fitch fits you properly?" she asked.

"It does indeed. They are finer garments than I am used to wearing. The tailor did a swell job."

"Molly has an excellent eye," she said. "Now then, Mr. Roosevelt told me only that you are aiding him on a matter of utmost national urgency. I am sure you will not let him down."

"I will do my best."

"That is all we can ask of anyone," she said. "By the by, when you see Mr. Roosevelt, please remind him that we are expecting company shortly."

From the way she said it, I reckoned she did not look forward to their visitor. "Excuse me, ma'am, do you know where the president is at this moment?"

"I suspect he is chopping wood."

"Chopping wood?"

"It is part of his plan for a strenuous life. Rather therapeutic. Even the Secret Servicemen keep their distance when he is in a Paul Bunyan mood."

"I see. Thank you, ma'am—for everything."

She waved her hand and I headed out.

I nearly stepped on a pair of knobby-kneed legs poking out of blue shorts as I made my way through the grove of locust trees.

"Hello," I said. The pale thirteen-year-old lifted his head. He had been reading Washington Irving's *The Sketchbook of Geoffrey Crayon, Gent.*, and continued to hold the book up, making it clear he preferred it to me. "Are you Kermit?"

"Yes. You must be the chap who is assisting my father. Mr. White?"

"Right."

"A pleasure to meet you, sir," he said, and returned his attention to the book.

Knowing I could not compete with Rip Van Winkle and Ichabod Crane, I made my way through the grove until I could hear the steady crack of the axe.

The sound grew louder as I approached, until it was almost like a gunshot. His jacket hung from a nearby tree in the grove of birches. His shirtsleeves were rolled up as he attacked a felled tree like it was a mortal enemy.

It was plain TR was a man who had used an axe and wedge before. Each blow struck the wood exactly as it should. But he was reducing the timber to kindling, muttering oaths as he split the pieces smaller and smaller. I figured it best not to bother him. And that is probably what saved his life.

There was a stump a couple of dozen yards from where the president was working, and I sat and watched. He was oblivious to me, a sign that he was truly upset. In general he was always aware of his surroundings. I was partially hidden by a thick clump of redberry evergreen bushes.

It was a good thing I was. If I had not been sitting there, if the sun had not been at that exact angle, if the sound of his axe on the wood had not put the thought of gunshots in my mind, if I had not had my new derringer loaded and within reach . . .

The sun coming through the trees glinted off a metal object in another clump of bushes on the far side of the president. I could think of nothing natural that would reflect like that. A few paces closer and I knew it was the barrel of a gun.

"Get down, Mr. Roosevelt!" I shouted, drawing my derringer. "What?"

I fired a tenth of a second before the figure in the bushes. His shot went wild.

The gunman rose up, bleeding from his left shoulder.

It was William Heinz of the Secret Service.

He drew a bead on the president. I am not a religious man, but I prayed for the Almighty to steady my hand as I fired.

The bullet hit Heinz in the chest, knocking him down before he could squeeze off another shot.

Mr. Roosevelt rushed over and propped Heinz's head up. "Go call for a doctor," he told me.

"I won't make it," Heinz said.

I stood frozen, wanting to hear the would-be assassin's last words.

"I am a loyal German."

"You are an American," Roosevelt said.

"I am a German first."

"Did the German government send you?"

Heinz gritted his teeth.

"It is time to make peace with this world. Why were you sent?"

Blood bubbled from his mouth when he tried to speak.

"Spike," Roosevelt said suddenly.

The dying man jumped as if he had been shot again. "How do you know?"

"Tell me the truth now. You have nothing to lose."

"He said you were planning to—guh—guh—planning to destroy the Fatherland." Heinz could tell us no more. His eyes rolled, he shuddered, and was gone.

"I owe you my life," TR said to me.

We were silent for a few moments. In the distance, I could hear shouting.

"Do you think Germany hired Spike? Or sent Heinz to kill you?" I asked.

He shook his head. "I doubt it. It would be foolish for them to kill me a half hour before their ambassador arrives."

"Morgan?"

"He is still on the road. For him too it would be more of a nuisance if I were to be killed right after exchanging words with him."

Marlowe raced up, coattails flying, buttoning his pants. He had the face of a thousand petty bureaucrats. Only the gun under his jacket gave away the fact that he was anything less than a middling, meddling paper pusher.

"What happened? Were those shots? What happened?" he asked. Seeing me with gun drawn, he finally thought to take out his own. Then he saw Heinz, and aimed at me. "Don't move!" he ordered.

"Put your gun away, Marlowe," TR ordered. "Jim just saved my life. From one of *your* men. Now listen closely. No one must know of this."

"But how?" Marlowe asked, lowering his gun but keeping it drawn. "There are reports to be filled, authorities to be—"

"I am not entirely without influence. With the help of the coroner, I think it can be arranged to appear as a hunting accident. Your report will show exactly that."

Four more Secret Servicemen appeared.

"But, but . . ." Marlowe sputtered.

"The assassin was under your command. Do you want that in the reports?"

A half dozen Secret Servicemen were closing in. All wanted to know what was going on.

"There's been a hunting accident," Marlowe said. "Everybody back to their posts. I'll make the arrangements."

By the time the freshly painted black carriage—with enough brass on it to make a mile-long banister—pulled up, TR was looking quite presidential, and not at all like a man who had just been an assassin's target.

From out of the carriage emerged a life-sized tin soldier, Baron Siegfried von Holleben. It was amazing that the tall, thin diplomat could hold his pear-shaped head up, since he had about twenty pounds of medals pinned to his red tunic.

I stood with the security men as the baron was received, keeping a close watch on the German's face and manner. Either von Holleben was an exceptional actor, or he wasn't at all surprised to see the president in perfect health. TR welcomed him as if nothing had happened. The two went off horseback riding while I assisted Marlowe and the Nassau County coroner in the removal of the late William Heinz.

By the time the men got back from their ride, O'Rourke had prepared a spectacular meal. It was the first time the entire family had sat together since my arrival.

Midway through the scrumptious eats, which included a fruit cocktail appetizer, roast beef, homegrown corn and spinach, I felt a hand on my thigh. To my left was Alice, who was chatting with the ambassador about Bavarian pastries. I pushed her hand away, but it quickly returned. There was a minor fracas under the table, until I noticed Mrs. Roosevelt watching.

"Are you sure your clothes fit properly?" she asked, seeing me fidgeting.

"Definitely, ma'am. I must have brushed against some poison ivy while walking."

"An old woodsman like you," TR said, chuckling.

The ambassador began a story about a hunting trip Emperor Franz Josef I of Austria had gone on near his lodge at Bad Ischl. As von Holleben boasted that the emperor had blasted more than thirty thousand animals in his time, Alice squeezed me in a spot that does not bear squeezing. I jumped.

"Perhaps you do not like the sport of hunting?" von Holleben asked me accusingly.

"If it serves a purpose." I had had a few glasses of wine to calm my nerves, and did not feel at all intimidated by the high-falutin' German. "I have no use for people who ride in trains and take potshots at the buffalo. They were here long before we were. The Indians make everything but rifles out of them."

"Fascinating," he said in a way that made it clear he did not think so.

I thought I saw a hint of smile on Mrs. Roosevelt's face.

The rest of the meal went well, except when Quentin threw a green bean at Archie.

Afterward, TR and the ambassador went to the library. I snuck down to the basement.

Their talk was about Venezuela, whose government had borrowed millions of dollars from Germany and Britain, then refused to pay up when the notes became due. The Europeans were threatening a blockade and possible attack if the Venzuelans did not make good.

Secretary of State John Hay had told the German there would be no objections from the United States, unless the Europeans tried to grab territory. From the way von Holleben and TR were talking, I figured the president was not so sure he wanted them in what he called our "sphere of influence."

There was lots of smart talk and I wondered if McFarlane was as savvy about politics as she was about finances. I could have used her to translate. I also wouldn't have minded another time alone with her in the basement.

"Spike," TR said abruptly.

"Vhat?"

"Spike."

"I do not understand," von Holleben said.

I couldn't see the German's face, but I knew from TR's tone that the baron had passed the test.

"I was just recalling the golden spike used at Promontory Point, Utah, to finish the transcontinental railroad in 1869," TR said, and gave a quick history.

I guess it drew suspicion from his belting out "spike," or at least the German was familiar enough with oddball behavior, especially by chiefs of state. Their talk turned to trifling matters. The candle was sputtering in its holder and I figured there wouldn't be anything else of interest.

I went upstairs to bed, remembering to lock my door. I went to sleep quite handily.

eight

By the time I awakened, the rest of the household, including von Holleben, had already enjoyed their breakfast. McFarlane and O'Rourke were cool to me, answering my greetings with nods and grunts, and not responding to my sociability. I felt like a kid who'd been caught with his hand in the cookie jar, only I didn't know what cookie jar I'd had my hand in.

After breakfast, Mrs. Roosevelt called me into her room. I fully expected to get my ears boxed.

"Theodore has told me what you did," she said. "I want to thank you."

"It was nothing."

"It was very brave of you. I hope you will stick by him."

"Through thick and thin."

"Well, as Theodore would say, 'Bully.'" With her few words and gestures, she had won me over in a big way.

I was feeling pretty chipper after I left her room until I saw McFarlane looking at me like a mother deer eyeing a wolf. I cornered her by the pantry. She was carrying a bundle of freshly washed towels. "What is the matter?"

She tried to wiggle by. "Excuse me, Mr. White."

"Then why the 'Mr. White'? I would think James, or perhaps even Jim."

"Maybe I should call you Fancy Dan."

I opened the pantry door and nudged her in. The scowl on her face and the armful of linen kept me from getting near. Surrounded by boxes of Borax and Pyle's Pearline Detergent, McFarlane and I got into a staring match. After what seemed like a decade I could take it no longer. I rolled my eyes and stuck out my tongue. I saw a hint of a thaw glimmering in those frigid blue eyes.

"It is one of the laws of these United States that even a condemned man gets to know the charges against him," I said. I held my neck sideways and pantomimed a rope around it. "Now, please tell me what it is I've done before you pull the trap out."

She finally told me that while tidying up my room she had found one of Alice's hairpins in my bed. I laughed. Audrey got even more peeved. When I told her the story of how the pin got there, she smiled.

"But I don't know how to corral her," I said. "I don't think I can talk to Mr. Roosevelt about it."

"You leave it to me."

"What will you do?"

"Let me put it this way: often the servants find out things they are not supposed to. Out of loyalty or good manners, they keep those matters to themselves. But tongues can wag at any time. I will talk to Alice."

"You're an angel," I said, giving her a peck on the lips. As she turned to leave, I patted her fanny.

"And you, Mr. White, are a devil." But her eyes were twinkling like the nighttime sky over Montana. "I must go fetch coffee for Mr. Roosevelt and his guest."

"Von Holleben?"

"No. He's left. The president has already seen two visitors. He has a very handsome gentleman in with him right now."

"And what business does this *handsome* fellow have with Mr. Roosevelt?"

"You're jealous," she said with a laugh.

"What about you and the cold shoulder you were giving me because of Alice?"

"A lady in a bedroom is different from a casual comment on a member of the opposite sex." She tapped me on the nose like I was a misbehaving mutt and bounced away.

I felt like a fool. Still, I had to see who had caught her eye. I wandered by TR's den.

"Jim, come in," TR said when he saw me.

I didn't understand why she thought the visitor was good-looking. He was a fop in a navy-blue worsted suit with a cherubic face and a small mustache under an aquiline nose. He had dark hair parted in the middle, thick lips, and large blue eyes.

"Jim, this is Brian Patterson. We had a few overlapping years at Harvard."

We shook hands. His grip was cold and ,clammy.

"A school friend. How nice," I said, trying to sound civil.

"Not really friends, old bean," Patterson said. "We know a lot of the same people. We both belonged to the better clubs. DKE, Hasty Pudding, Porcellian. You know how it is."

"I can't say I do," I said.

"Brian came here with a warning," TR said.

"I don't mean to be impertinent," Patterson said. "I'm sure your own men are quite up to the task. How many Secret Service guards do you have anyway?"

"I never counted. More than I need," TR said.

Patterson asked me if I was a security man. I looked to TR, who said, "No. Jim's just a friend. Why don't you tell him what you heard."

"Very well, old chum," Patterson said. "I've been running my father's steamship line in Boston. That necessitates quite a lot of work at the docks. You can imagine the sorts I encounter.

"Anyway, I've heard from some terribly disreputable sources, people who know about such things, that there is a plot afoot to get Teddy, I mean, President Roosevelt, out of office. By hook or by crook."

I bombarded him with questions, but he had no answers. He said he was keeping an ear open and had volunteered to supply some of his own security men, all vouched for with the highest credentials, to help out.

"I'm most touched, Brian," TR said. "I must, however, decline your offer. I will keep it in mind if things heat up."

The men began reminiscing about old times at school, and TR tried to catch up on the exploits of alumni he knew. After a few more minutes, Patterson made for the door.

"What do you think of old Brian?" TR asked in the few minutes we had alone before his next appointment.

"I don't like him. When he was leaving, he looked like a burglar casing a house for his next job."

"That stickpin he was wearing was worth more than my presidential salary," TR said with a chuckle. "The ring on his finger probably even more. Did you notice it?"

"Of course," I said, though I hadn't.

"Don't be put off by Patterson's manner. Lots of the chaps at Harvard were like that. Their hearts are in the right place, even if their noses are in the air," TR said. "Now, you better head out before my next visitor. He's the state senator from Montauk, and a more arrogant and blockheaded boor would be hard to find."

I took a few steps toward the door.

"Jim," TR said. "Don't let this conspiracy business weigh too heavily on your shoulders. A year of worrying is less productive than a minute of action."

Out on the broad porch I rested my bones in a rocker. I dozed off. When I awoke, I laid eyes on a wallet lying near the rail.

Who could've dropped it? Heinz? The ambassador? Morgan? Patterson? I got up and reached for it. The wallet moved. I grabbed, and missed again. As I made a frantic lunge, I saw the string attached.

"Fooled you, fooled you," Quentin yelled, appearing from his hiding place underneath the porch.

"Why you little rascal," I bellowed in mock rage, making as if to seize him. He shouted and raced across the field with more energy than a litter of puppies.

"He is quite rambunctious," said Kermit, who had approached as quiet as an Indian scout.

"Has Ichabod Crane met the Headless Horseman yet?"

"I finished that. I am halfway through *The Last of the Mohicans.*"

"That was a humdinger. Your father loaned it to me once, along with *The Deerslayer.*"

He started talking about Natty Bumppo, the Daniel Boone legend, Rousseau's natural man, and American manhood. It was quite a conversation to have with a thirteen-year-old. After a few minutes, I felt I was over my head.

"I would love to continue our talk," I said. "But I better go speak with your father."

The president was reviewing papers at his desk in the Gun Room. He took off his glasses and gave them a quick buff. "What avenue of investigation did you expect to follow next?" TR asked.

"I planned to poke around New York a bit."

He set the papers down. "Bully. Will we be pursuing new leads, or following up on established ones?"

Putting the president back in the line of fire was the last thing I wanted. I tried to convince him to stay at Sagamore Hill, but his mind was made up.

"Before we go, there's something you should know," he said. "That man who visited me this morning was not Brian Patterson."

"What?"

"Patterson has been out of the country for six months. I checked by telephone," TR explained.

"Who do you think it was?"

TR shrugged. "Someone trying to wheel a Trojan horse into my fort. If this whole affair wasn't so serious, it would be manly sport, eh, Jim? I suppose the vital nature of this business is what makes it so stimulating." He hesitated. I had the feeling he was trying to decide whether he should tell me something important. But he chose not to. When he spoke, it was to explain how we could get away.

TR and his boys and their friends often rowed across Oyster Bay and camped out overnight. Mr. Roosevelt let it be known that he and I would be doing that.

Marlowe wanted to send along some of his security men, but the president said no. Marlowe looked at me like I was a side-winder. I guess I couldn't blame him. Since I'd showed up, the president had gotten secretive with everybody, and come back from a jaunt looking like he'd gotten a good shellacking. I'd saved TR's life, but in a way that was doubly embarassing to Marlowe.

The Secret Service chief wasn't the only one who didn't approve. Archie and Quentin glared like I'd stolen their best friend. Alice had a sullen pout, Mrs. Roosevelt a worried look.

When Audrey got me alone, she kissed me and whispered, "Go with God."

TR insisted on doing the lion's share of the rowing. While he pulled, he said how he thought there could be war with Germany and possibly England because of this Venezuela thing. Von Holleben had spoken in what the president said was a threatening manner.

A gull swooped, nearly brushing our heads. TR began talking about the possibility of flight by heavier-than-air machines. We were in a race with the Germans to be the first off the ground. "One day, wars will be fought in the skies with great fighting machines swooping and attacking like goshawks after starlings. America will be at the forefront."

"How far up the road will this be?"

"I can tell you, Jim, and this is in the strictest confidence, that even as we speak, two brothers in North Carolina are developing an aeroplane that will give man the freedom the birds have enjoyed since time immemorial. I receive weekly updates by courier."

He said the brothers—bicycle repairmen by trade—had set up shop at Kitty Hawk, where sea breezes helped the gliders and sand dunes cushioned the failures.

We landed at Oyster Bay. Several Secret Servicemen landed nearby. But TR was prepared. He led them on a merry chase, through a field, into a forest, and then left them stuck in a bramble patch.

We went to another hideaway barn, and from the picnic basket TR took a disguise kit. He padded himself until he was as round as Grover Cleveland. He put on a curly gray wig, a bushy beard, a checked golf cap, and elevated shoes. When he was through, he had added two inches to his five-foot, eight-inch frame, and fifty pounds to the two hundred he carried.

He offered me a bushy mustache and matching eyebrows, which

I attached with rubber cement. He gave me a derby and clear-glass spectacles. I put flesh-colored greasepaint over my mouse.

"Now, let us see what Aguilar has to say," TR said.

But Aguilar would tell no one anything. Late the day before someone had set fire to his mattress while he was asleep. By the time guards had answered his screams, it was too late.

The toothpick-chewing guard who told us was annoyed at Aguilar for causing trouble by his death. "He musta been been talking to somebody he shouldn'ta been," the guard said. "So the other animals roasted him. Then us guards gotta do extra work. Clean up the mess the animals make. We oughtta just let them kill themselves off. Save the money."

"I demand to see the warden," TR said, forgetting our roles.

The guard was amused. "How would you like to see the inside of a cell? For thirty days?"

"Excuse my friend here," I said. "He's very upset. Raoul owed us quite a piece of change."

The guard nodded. An unpaid debt was something he could understand.

"Raoul was involved in a business venture with us, in which he failed to pay his share," TR explained.

"What did you do, rob a bank together?"

I just smiled and took out a silver dollar. I began tossing it in the air. The guard's eyes locked on it.

"You could be very helpful by letting us take a gander at his file," I said.

The guard looked around and made sure no one was in earshot. "That sounds like five dollars worth of helpfulness to me."

I paid up.

The guard fetched the file and led us to a small interrogation room. "Five minutes. That's all you get," he said, handing over the file and shutting the door.

TR laid the file on the small pine table, took the pocket watch from his vest, and checked it. We began to read.

Raoul Aguilar, the black sheep of a prosperous Colombian shipping family, had been sent up north to prevent disgrace to his family. This information was provided confidentially by the Colombian ambassador. I noticed that TR's eyes widened, and then narrowed, when he read about the Colombian connection. I filed that under my hat for future investigation.

Aguilar was an opium addict, who quickly ran through his allowance. Using his swarthy good looks, he had seduced a slew of girls into becoming scarlet women and had been arrested by police in New York and Boston. For all his New York offenses, he was represented by a lawyer named Lancaster Clay.

"Most intriguing," TR said, tapping the name. "I know Clay. He is active in Democratic politics of the lower sort. A Tammany minion I encountered during my anti-corruption campaign as—"

The door opened. "Your time is up," the guard said, reaching over and grabbing the file.

We rose. "Thanks for your help," I said. "What's you name?"

"Why?" he asked suspiciously.

"My partner and I might have some business back here. If we don't see you, we want to know who to ask for. It will be good for everyone," I said with a wink.

"They call me Turk."

By the time we reached Clay's office—right behind Brooklyn Borough Hall on Joralemon Street—we had a plan: I would go in and rile up Clay. When Clay came running out to check on the story I told him, we would follow in a cab TR had gotten.

I entered the wood-frame building. The green paint on the shutters matched the lettering on the sign: LANCASTER CLAY, ESQ., ATTORNEY-AT-LAW, NO LEGAL MATTER TOO TROUBLESOME.

His heavily made-up secretary had a wayward smile. "Can I help you?" she asked.

"I must see Mr. Clay," I said, removing my hat.

Behind her a closed door was marked with a sign, PRIVATE.

"He's a busy man. If you would like to make an appointment?"

"I must see him now," I said, taking a few steps forward.

"You touch that door, buster, and you spend the night at Raymond Street," she said, sounding like she could hold her own on any waterfront.

"Tough talk from a little lady."

"I can back it up," she said. "Mr. Clay has lots of friends in high places."

"I know. I am here at the behest of one of them."

"Who?"

"I have a message for him alone. He'd best not hear that you turned me away."

"Who are you?"

I put my hat back on. "My name is Mickey. I work for Silent Charlie."

Invoking the name of Charles Murphy, the Tammany boss, did wonders to improve her estimation of me.

"Why didn't you say so?"

She spoke into a mouthpiece.

"What is it?" a tinny voice asked through the horn.

"A representative of Mr. Murphy."

"Send him in."

I smiled at her, she smiled back, and I walked into Clay's inner office.

The wood-paneled room smelled of sweet pipe tobacco. The source of the odor was a meerschaum in the mouth of Lancaster

Clay. He puffed away, looking real pleased with himself. "How is Silent Charlie?" he asked.

"Fine. Watching out for the public's interests as he usually does."

"And his wife and children?"

I wasn't sure that Murphy had a wife and children, and sensed a possible trap.

"I'm in a hurry, Mr. Clay, not here on a social call."

"I see."

"I came here about Raoul Aguilar."

He nearly swallowed a cloud of smoke. Clay walked to the window, which faced the courthouse. He stared out at the elegant domed building. Puffs rose from his pipe like smoke from an Indian camp fire. I couldn't see his face.

"I am not sure I know such a person."

"You were his attorney. Don't play me for a chowderhead."

"Who sent you?"

"Silent Charlie. He got a tip from Turk."

"At the jail?"

"Where else. He told me I could pick up some spending money by bringing you a message."

"What is it?"

"It will cost you a double eagle."

"That's a lot of money. What is it about?"

"I told you. Aguilar."

"He's dead."

I turned and took two steps toward the door. "I understood you to be smart, a team player. Maybe we just do things different across the river."

"All right, all right." He went to his desk and dug a gold coin from the bottom drawer. Since it seemed to be the thing to do, I tested the coin by biting into it.

"You don't trust me?"

"I don't trust my own mother," I said, pocketing it. "Elsewise, why would she have given birth to a rascal like me? Anyway, you should know there were two men by the jail today asking about Aguilar. Turk put them off the scent. For the moment."

"Where were they from?" he asked nervously.

"*The Daily Eagle.*"

"Damn. I'll have to speak to the editor about his reporters snooping about. What were their names? What did they look like?"

I said I didn't know their names and described a duo nothing like the president and me.

He returned to his desk and refilled the bowl of his pipe. He was so wrapped up in his thoughts, he didn't answer my good-bye.

I found the president waiting around the corner with a cab driver who had a bushy head of hair the same color as his roan mare. He clearly spent more money on his horse than himself.

"This waiting time is costing you swells money," the driver said as he climbed atop his cab.

We nodded.

"Do you think Clay believed you?" TR asked when the driver was out of earshot.

"It doesn't matter. He knows something is going on with Aguilar or I wouldn't have visited."

In five minutes, Clay ran from his building, coattails flying, pipe in his teeth, and top hat on his head. A cab pulled up and he hopped in.

"Follow that cab," TR said.

Clay's first stop was the Raymond Street jail.

"Well, now he knows I'm not who I said I was." I peeled the mustache from my face.

We followed Clay down Adams Street, then over the bridge into Manhattan.

"This great city has for too long been infected with insidious corruption," TR said. "Ever since Peter Minuet thought he got a bargain by buying the island for twenty-four dollars, when in fact the sellers were not the owners, its denizens have prided themselves on their cunning.

"The Tammany sachems are the worst of the lot. If there is one group that I could safely say wishes me ill, it is the heirs of Boss Tweed."

Then Clay's carriage stopped, he hopped out, and ran up the stairs into 52 Chambers Street—the Tweed courthouse, a monument to graft and a den of TR's enemies.

nine

Since his first days of public service, the president had chipped away at the kind of graft the Tammany pols thrived on—kickbacks, boondoggles, bribery, extortion, freeloading, nepotism, influence peddling, favoritism, featherbedding. Despite his work, New York still had more corrupt cops, politicians, and judges than a barrel cactus has thorns.

We paid the cab driver and followed Clay up the great entrance stairs at a discreet distance.

"Do you know one carpenter received $360,747 for a month's work on the building? Some plasterer earned, and I use that word loosely, $2,870,464 for nine months?" TR growled.

We waded through the stream of people going into the building. This was the place where justice was bought and sold. There was the noisy bustle of a train station inside the hall as wardheelers, alderman, and other cunning types mixed with the more obvious criminals, to pick up tips on the best ways to cheat their fellow man. The president was squinting and baring his teeth. Fortunately, most of the criminals were scowling too, and he fit right in.

He named the rogue's around us: Leaning against a pillar was

Monk Eastman, who had circulated a price list of strong-arm services. Leg breaking cost three dollars, murder was five dollars and up. Moving like a king through his court was Judge Randolph Sullivan, considered extremely honest because once he was bought, he stayed bought. He was one of several members of Big Tim Sullivan's clan serving on the bench. Big Tim was Timothy Daniel Sullivan, congressman and vice lord of the East Side. TR said he made more than five million a year through prostitution, illegal-boxing promotion, gambling dens, bars, liquor distribution, and partnership in the Sullivan and Considine vaudeville circuit.

"I fought so many of these rapscallions," TR said. "Brushing against them reminds me of the parasites in the Cuban swamps."

I flinched at the memory of the two-inch-long black leeches that would cling for a meal until tapped with a cigarette or slug of alcohol.

The smoke from Clay's pipe made him as visible as a locomotive chugging up a mountain grade. He wended his way through the horde, shaking an occasional hand here, patting a back there, but clearly a man with a mission.

He reached his target, a man of about forty with a huge body and a head that seemed to have been added on as an afterthought. His mouth—ringed by a dirty-looking blond beard—hung slack, giving him an ignorant look.

"Is that—"

"Yes," TR said. "He was one of our assailants from the waterfront."

Clay mumbled a few sentences to the thug, who grew angrier with each word. We were standing about twenty-five feet away, too far to hear anything in the noisy crowd. Clay looked very happy when he finally got away from the glaring goon.

"Do we follow him?" TR asked, indicating Clay with a nod of his head.

"I think he has delivered the message."

"I agree. We should trail our friend from yesterday. We do owe him something," TR said, with a grin that reminded me of Quentin's, right before he pulled some bit of mischief.

Stalking a man is not much different from stalking an animal. You stay upwind, out of sight, and blend in with the surroundings. No sudden moves, hang back, and wait until the right time to move in for the kill.

We followed our attacker uptown on the Broadway streetcar and then east on the Fourteenth Street line. He didn't pay his five-cent fare for either trip and neither conductor challenged him. We had picked up newspapers and used them to shield our faces as we stood at opposite ends of the car.

"We can allow the grizzly a longer leash," TR said as we got out of the trolley and headed north on Second Avenue. "I know where we are going. Charlie's Place at Second Avenue and Twenty-first Street."

I knew the name of the saloon from articles I had read in the Hearst papers. The bar was one of three watering holes owned by Charles Francis "Silent Charlie" Murphy, the forty-four-year-old Tammany machine chief. TR said Murphy had risen to power despite not being a backslapper like his predecessors. The man who had been described as dull and dumb controlled ninety thousand precinct workers under thirty-five district leaders.

We followed our quarry into the lion's den. There was no turning back. The noisy bar was crowded with stevedores, liverymen, gashouse workers, and assorted laborers, come to enjoy a schooner of beer and a bowl of soup for five cents, with free crackers, cheese, and bologna. Even more important, Murphy was known for not serving women, who were leaving the home and wrecking the atmosphere of groggeries.

Our man elbowed through the crowd and went up a flight of stairs. We stopped at the bar and paid our nickels. The beer was good, the soup, some sort of chicken-and-barley concoction, was hot and greasy.

"I'm going up. Wait here," I said, taking off before TR had a chance to argue.

I climbed the stairs to the second floor, where a sign read ANAWANDA CLUB. I strutted in.

"What is it?" demanded a gent who sat at the door. He looked like he drank his beer by the barrelful and had taken on that shape as a result.

"I want a job," I said, my eyes roving around the room.

"So does everybody and his brother," the barrel man said, looking up from his copy of *Argosy.*

"I'm prepared to work for it."

"How?"

"I used to be the best repeater on the West Side. Vote Early and Often Jones, they called me."

"Can you sign your name?"

"Not only my name, but that of half the dear departed in Greenwood Cemetery."

"When Mister Murphy is free, I'll see if we can use you."

Beer Barrel returned his attention to the magazine. I moseyed into the room. At the far side, there was an open door to an office. Inside, I saw my man, and he was with Charles Francis Murphy himself. I sidled close. Although the dozen or so men in the meeting room were making huzza-huzza noises, I could hear a not-so-Silent Charlie and his guest because their voices were raised in anger.

". . . and Big Tim will be the ruin of this organization," Murphy said. He was seated with his back to a rolltop desk that held a stack of papers under a tiger paperweight. He was a jowly, ruddy-faced man with the severe expression of an indignant librarian.

"But Mr. Murphy, we did not—"

"Listen, Jake, you always act without thinking, so don't say you didn't know. If Sullivan wants to run brothels or gambling dens, he had better learn how to do it discreetly. If he wants you to do strong-arm favors, he had better make sure it doesn't bounce back on us.I always said dealing with Spike was like dealing with the devil. Now you tell me there's a mess brewing over in Brooklyn because you and . . ."

Murphy looked over in my direction. I made as if I was studying a photograph on the wall of the Anawanda baseball team. He got up and shut the door. Powerful men slamming doors in my face seemed to be becoming a trend.

I drifted across the room, waiting until Beer Barrel wasn't paying attention. When it was clear, I sidled past him and back downstairs. What I saw from the landing made my heart sink to my feet. A rowdy crowd had gathered around the spot where I had left the president.

I took the stairs two at a time, imagining what had happened. He had gotten into a to-do with some regular and was being stomped like a grape by the mob.

Mr. Roosevelt was at the center of the crowd. But he was standing quite naturally, back against the bar. "No man can be a good citizen unless he has a wage more than sufficient to cover the cost of living, and hours of labor short enough so that after his day's work is done he will have time and energy left over," TR said.

The crowd cheered.

"Everyone is entitled to a square deal, young and old, rich and poor, Catholic and Protestant, workingman and magnate. America is the greatest nation on the face of the earth, and as the Constitution guarantees, every citizen is entitled to life, liberty, and the pursuit of happiness."

I elbowed my way to TR. "Vote for Honest Archie Quentin for alderman," I yelled. "Hip, hip . . ."

"Hooray."

"Hip, hip . . ."

"Hooray."

"Drinks are on Silent Charlie," I said.

Cheers as everyone bellied up to the bar. The confused barkeep began setting them up and looking to the stairs for some sort of confirmation. I clamped TR's elbow and eased him out, although every thick-armed galoot in the place wanted to pat his back or shake his hand.

I was just finishing telling TR what I had overheard when Jake came lumbering out. We followed him a few blocks. Up ahead, we could see a deserted construction site.

"I'm afraid we can't pursue him all day," TR said. "What say we ask him a few questions?"

Before I could answer, TR took off running, catching up with Jake in front of the site. I got there just in time to hear him call Jake "a great wart on Silent Charlie's behind."

Jake swung wildly. TR dodged the blow and ran behind the wooden site fence with Jake on his heels. I followed them. When he saw the two of us, he said, "You picked the wrong guy to rob."

TR waved for me to stand back. I kept my hand on the gun, but obeyed. Jake took out a billy club and lunged at TR. Without his friends and the element of surprise, he was no match for the pugilistic president.

TR ducked under Jake's swing and landed a right and left hook to Jake's abdomen. The big man stood frozen, gasping for air. Three jabs, and then an uppercut, and Jake was flat on his back.

I went over and pulled Jake up by his dirty blond hair. "You better answer some questions, quick, or I turn my friend loose on you," I said. "My chum is a killer and he's madder than hell."

Jake couldn't see me wink at TR. But the president picked up my cue. He growled and gnashed his teeth like a ferocious beast.

"Just keep him away," Jake said, a coward when it came to receiving, instead of giving, pain.

"We know all about you," I said. "One lie, and my friend here uses you for a punching bag again."

"Tell us about Spike," TR snarled.

"You know about him?"

"Grrrh," TR said, surging forward. I blocked him, as if to stop him from destroying Jake.

"Spike hired me and a few of the boys to go work over these nosy mugs. I don't know why. Honest."

"What about Silent Charlie? Or Big Tim?" I asked.

"They didn't know about it. I was just picking up some extra coin, you know, times is tough."

"What do you know about Raoul Aguilar?"

"I don't know nuthin'. Honest, honest I don't."

With me playing the gentleman, and TR the bad guy, we continued to question Jake. He said he'd heard Spike had left the city and was in Washington D.C. He did not know who Spike was working for.

"Okay, Jake, now you keep your mouth shut and we won't tell anyone you squealed," I said. I led TR away, much to Jake's relief.

"Gad, that was dee-lightful. Tomorrow I must return to Washington. I wonder if my play-acting can help quicken my transactions with the scalawags on Capitol Hill."

With that, he burst out laughing.

"This hasn't changed much since I was here," TR said, as he surveyed the high-ceilinged office in police headquarters on Mulberry Street.

The man sitting in a cane swivel chair behind the large oak desk nodded. His name was Roderick Burnson and he held the rank of captain. The jut-jawed, deepset-eyed Irishman headed the New York Police Department's criminal information unit. TR and me, in disguise, had snuck into his office, using a back stairway TR remembered. Burnson, who recognized the president instantly, had said almost nothing since our arrival. I thought he was angry.

"There's a blackguard named Spike operating in the city," TR said, outlining the little we knew about him.

Burnson nodded and walked out.

"Not a very friendly copper," I said.

"Rod? Being an honest man in a pack of thieves makes a man taciturn. He's a manly fellow and a fine officer to boot."

TR told me how he had found Burnson patroling a beat in Staten Island because he'd refused to take part in a ring of officers shaking down bars that were staying open on Sunday. Mr. Roosevelt had chosen Burnson as a sidekick when he went undercover looking for corrupt coppers. He recounted a few of their adventures, chuckling merrily, and said it was a sign of positive change that Burnson could rise to such an important position in the NYPD.

I was disappointed when I saw how slim the file was that Burnson returned with. He handed it to TR. The president read it, then passed it to me. The report was written in that funny language police use, with lots of "observed the perpetrators" sprinkled in. What it said was that Spike's real name, birthplace, and details about his background were unknown. He was described only as a dark-haired white man in his fifties.

According to a reliable informant, Spike had been a crook since his teens, active in fencing goods stolen off docked ships and pimping women to sailors. In later years, he had branched out into labor racketeering. He worked for either union or management, depending on which side offered more money. He was suspected of involvement in at least seventeen murders. He had never been arrested.

A second stoolie confirmed the information, adding only that Spike had recently shown signs of the tertiary stage of syphilis. He had brief seizures and bouts of violent insanity. He was known to have assaulted two men during these fits. His lunacy hadn't affected his criminal cunning. His operation included several dozen men and women. The informants were only able to produce aliases for the associates, which proved to be untraceable.

"I have one thing to add," Burnson said when I looked up. "Informant two was found dead shortly after providing us with information."

"Was he killed because he informed?" TR asked.

"Yes."

"How can you be positive?" I asked.

"He was found with a spike nailed through his tongue."

ten

I've gotten around this country in a lot of different ways. I've worn out shoe leather walking and the seat of my pants riding horseback. I've hopped freights and ridden the rails, as well as being a paying customer on passenger lines. But nothing beat the ride I got in the president's own train, a true land yacht.

It only had three cars, behind a big black E–2, 4–4–2 Atlantic steam locomotive. With the eighty-inch driving wheels, and a throttle artist in the cab, it could do better than a hundred miles an hour.

The Pullman nearest the engine was for staff, which included Marlowe; Bill Craig and two other Secret Servicemen; O'Rourke; Miss Young, the children's tutor; William Loeb, Mr. Roosevelt's secretary; and Audrey. The second car was for the family. The third car was for Mr. Roosevelt.

The staff car was more comfortable than any regular train running, but the other two cars were miracles of modern transportation.

In the second car, there were plush sofas, love seats, and rockers of Turkish leather. Tasseled yellow-velvet curtains capped the plate-glass windows. Illumination from electric lighting gleamed off the polished brass rails and fixings. It looked like a showplace parlor from a magazine. Audrey proudly pointed out the furnishings like they were her own. The seventy-five-foot-long car was divided into three sections. There was also a kitchen area and small bathrooms.

Mr. Roosevelt's car had top-quality furnishings too, but was more Spartan. A mahogany desk and chairs glowed with a reddish-brown finish. There was a stuffed mountain lion in a corner and a grandfather clock facing his desk. A boxing bag hung at the far end of the car. A moose head and a few guns were on one wall.

I had free run of the train. However, when I entered the president's Pullman, Loeb, a thin, precise man, gave me a look as clear as a Do Not Disturb sign. TR was pacing the floor, dictating a memo about "land reclamation." I moved on to the family car.

I found a small, deserted compartment and a copy of the latest issue of *McClure's*. Ida Tarbell was giving John D. Rockefeller his comeuppance in a series of articles.

Just as I was settling down, I heard Miss Young say, "All right children, you may go and stretch your legs," and the next thing I knew, Archie and Quentin charged in. They shot spitballs out the window until Mrs. Roosevelt came and gave them a chewing out. They stopped and turned their attention to me. After jumping in and out of my lap like pigs in a mud puddle, Archie got a toy rubber sword and Quentin a mask. They ran around me wildly, playing St. George and the dragon.

I made them a deal. If they would leave me alone, I'd tell them about some of TR's and my adventures. I recited a couple of stories and they finally took off.

I had only a few minutes' peace and quiet before Alice sauntered into the compartment and pulled down the curtain. She lit a cigarette.

"That is an unpleasant habit for a lady," I told her.

101

She inhaled deeper and exhaled longer, then stuck out her tongue and blew a perfect smoke ring before flouncing out.

Kermit came in and asked what I knew about Groton. He said he would be going there shortly and hoped he could cut the mustard. I told him I thought he was quite a scholar. I returned to *McClure's*, while he read Socrates.

Then Ethel joined us, holding a small stuffed bear under one arm and eating an apple. "What are you reading?" she asked, fixing me with deep blue eyes.

I showed her.

"My daddy is good friends with the editor. He comes to the house often."

"Shhhhh," Kermit said. "We are trying to read."

"A gentleman does not speak that way to a lady, Kermit Roosevelt," she said. "If you do not treat me properly, I will punch you in the nose."

She told me the stuffed animal, called a "Teddy Bear," had been sent to her from a Brooklyn candy store. She said her father had been hunting in Mississippi when others in his party cornered a black bear on its last legs. They offered the bear to TR to shoot. He said no to the unsportsmanlike trophy. Newspapermen picked up the story and had a field day. The toy bears became popular, cleverly marketed by the candy-store owner, who renamed his business Ideal Toys.

The two youngest barged in, having just finished wrestling with their father on the carpeted floor of his office. If only Mr. Edison could have harnessed their energy, he would have powered all the lights in New York.

I wandered out to see Audrey, who was hard at work with Mrs. Roosevelt. During our brief chat, she explained that many of the previous administrations had been slapdash with the taxpayers' property. Mrs. R wanted to make sure the American people and the future First Families could enjoy their heritage, so they were inventorying the White House property.

I peeked into Mr. Roosevelt's car. He was talking intently to Craig. Loeb was nowhere in sight. I decided that anything fit for the Secret Serviceman's ears was fit for mine and walked in.

"Jim, glad you're here," TR said. "I have been thinking long and hard about it, and I concluded I must share my suspicions with both of you."

"What?" I sputtered. "All along, you've said our work must be kept secret. I can't believe that, I don't understand, how could you let someone else in on it? Why tell him?"

TR frowned. "Excuse me, Bill," he said to the Secret Serviceman. Craig walked to the far side of the car and looked out the window.

"That was intolerably rude," TR scolded me. "Not only did it insult Mr. Craig, but it questioned my judgment. I have known Bill Craig since I was governor. I trust him implicitly."

"But why tell him? He could just follow orders."

"I respect his opinion and need him to make decisions based on knowledge, not guesses," TR snapped.

"But we were—"

"We were fine in Sagamore. Washington is different. Many people will have access to me and my family. If you and I are pursuing one lead, I cannot be fearful that our quarry is doubling back and hitting me where I am most vulnerable. If anything were to happen to Edith or the children, I would never forgive myself."

I said nothing.

TR took off his glasses, buffed them, and put them back on. "Bill is a manly fellow, the kind we can depend on. My mind is made up. If you cannot make peace with the thought, let me know now."

"He will do," I said.

TR gestured to Craig and the Secret Serviceman returned.

"The canal across the Isthmus—have you been reading about the situation in the newspapers?" TR asked us.

"I know there has been talk about it for years," I said, "Through Nicaragua."

"No longer Nicaragua—too many volcanoes and earthquakes. Panama is now the most practical location. The trip from New York to San Francisco would be cut by seven thousand, eight hundred miles if a ship could travel through a canal across the Isthmus. But Panama is controlled by Colombia, and that government of contemptible blackguards thinks they can trifle with the United States."

TR was out from behind his desk, pacing and pounding his fist into his hand. "Secretary of State Hay worked out problems with the French company that owned rights to build the canal. We bought that license for forty million dollars."

He stomped out of the room to the rear platform. Craig and I followed. The president was looking out at the world we were racing by as the train clickety-clacked through the Maryland countryside. A family stood waiting at a crossing. When they saw whose train it was, they waved frantically. TR waved back, no less vigorously.

"Hay came to an amicable agreement with a Colombian representative," TR continued. "Ten million initially and a quarter of a million each year in rent. The Colombian legislature now is balking. Blackmail, I call it. Extortion of the lowest sort."

Seeing Craig standing next to him, I felt ornery. I did something I could never imagine myself doing. I debated politics with the president. "It sounds as if the French company got a much better deal than the country where the canal is to be built."

"A deal is a deal, and if a man is a man, he stands by his word," TR responded. "Panama will become the center of a major trade route, which will no doubt benefit their economy."

"Who was this person who Secretary Hay had the deal with? Did he have the right to strike a bargain?" I asked.

"He was an *authorized* representative," TR barked.

"Why is this so important?" I challenged.

"If you would stop interrupting, I could tell you," TR said. "You remember Aguilar, and how that poor youngster told us about him meeting with Spanish gentlemen?"

"Yes."

"I suspect those men were Colombians. I believe Spike is working for Colombia."

"Just because we are trying to get a bargain on the canal, you think they would dare stage an attack on the president of the United States?" I asked.

We passed another crossing. One of those horseless carriages was parked, waiting for us to pass. The couple in it regarded our train as nothing more than an obstacle. Mr. Roosevelt frowned. Looking disappointed, he paced back and forth on the small rear platform for a while and then returned to the car. He glanced from me to Craig and then back again, as if weighing our mettle.

"In a short period of time, things will be happening in Panama. I cannot elaborate. Perhaps the Colombians have gotten wind of a surprise I have in store for them." The president spoke slowly, careful with every word. I could only think of one possibility. War.

TR went back to his desk and burrowed into his papers. Craig stood next to me on the rear platform. The landscape streaked by.

"I hope he did not mean what I think he means," Craig said, and I nodded. "It is good that you have the courage to question him," he said. "He is lucky to have a friend like you."

I watched Craig through jealous eyes, not sure if he was as good-hearted as he pretended to be, or a spy planted in our midst. Then the train whistle blew and we were in the capital of these forty-five United States.

A crowd of several hundred was waiting as we pulled into Union Station. They waved flags and whooped it up. A Marine Corps band struck up the president's favorite song, the Rough Rider theme, "A Hot Time in the Old Town Tonight."

What a thrill! What an honor! What a worry. I wondered how prophetic the song would be as the president walked to the railing at the rear of his car and waved to cheering crowds.

My first few days in Washington, D.C., were overwhelming, kind of like the first time I saw the Grand Canyon, or New York harbor, or a naked woman.

The District, as I soon found people called it, had been the nation's capital for a little over a hundred years. But like everything else Mr. Roosevelt touched, he changed it for the better.

Actually, the change had been started by his predecessor. To make a plan for the city, McKinley had appointed Senator James McMillan, architect David Burnham, architect Charles F. McKim—who also helped renovate the White House, but more on that shortly—landscape artist Frederick Law Olmsted—who had done wonders with New York's Central Park—and Augustus Saint-Gaudens—a famous sculptor whom TR later commissioned to design coins. New federal buildings, re-landscaping the mall, and waterfront parks by the Tidal Basin were part of the beautification project.

I knew all this because I had the best and prettiest guide in the District. We toured the Capitol Building, climbed the 555-foot Washington Monument, rode on the C & O Canal barge over in Georgetown, and visited the red-brick Smithsonian Institution.

Audrey polished my manners on which fork to eat with, what a finger bowl was for, and the importance of putting a napkin on my lap before I chowed down. She also identified various dignitaries and told me their pedigrees. I had time for the education because the president had insisted I not investigate without him, and he was wrapped up in official business. Let's see how good a job Bill Craig does, I thought.

It turned out Craig did an excellent job. While he was watching the president I got stuck with the children. They came with Audrey and me during our travels around town. Although she had almost as much control over them as their mother, I would have preferred being with TR to playing nursemaid.

I had been concerned that I'd be ignored and feel out of place in the capital. But I gained importance after TR introduced me as "his special friend and advisor." Word spread faster than a brush fire through tinder-dry grass, and soon, even without TR around, I was paid attention to.

It was harder for me to see the president, though. All sorts of people and projects were taking up his time. One of the biggest things on his mind was the wide-open spaces.

TR had appointed Gifford Pinchot head of the forestry service, which was quite a change, since previously it had been run by bureaucrats who wouldn't know a sparrow from a screech owl. Pinchot had grand notions about irrigating the West. He was a strapping gent, a scholar about forests and deserts and such. The president told me Pinchot had begun bending his ear even before McKinley's body was cold in the ground. He convinced TR to make irrigation a priority and pushed through Congress the Reclamation Act, whereby public lands were sold and the money used to irrigate desert. The newly watered property was sold to settlers. There were twenty-eight projects to irrigate three million acres, with seven thousand miles of canals, brand new bridges, reservoirs, and higher dams than had ever been made before.

John Muir, the other great nature-lover, was adding his two cents, by mail, pushing for the protection of land in California and Alaska. The funny thing was that Muir and Pinchot did not get along. Muir was a naturalist, which meant he wanted things left natural. Pinchot was a conservationist, which meant he would go for limited development, as long as they didn't wreck hell out of the place. Both men lobbied as aggressively as missionaries.

That was a popular word in Washington—lobbying. You would have thought it had something to do with a hotel lobby, and maybe it once did. It meant arm-twisting, begging, bribing, charming, convincing someone in power to do what you wanted.

Since Theodore Roosevelt was the most powerful man in government everyone tried to lobby him, from old soldiers wanting their Civil War records improved, to European diplomats, who wanted to make sure the United States remained an ally, or at least neutral, as they went about intriguing against each other.

Another popular word was "reception," which was the Washington way of saying "party." For folks serious about the business of running a country, they sure did like to cut the rug. A couple of times a week, the Roosevelts played host. Most every night some ambassador, senator, or lobbyist was throwing a bash.

TR told me to attend as many receptions as I could. "This is a town which thrives on gossip and the barter of information. You are of more value to me out mingling than sitting with me like a shepherd watching his flock." I was fitted for a couple of fancy suits and suitable accessories for a gentleman. Dressed in a black monkey suit, Audrey said I was quite a man about town.

I had free run of the White House. Walking down hallways where great leaders strolled gave me a jolt. The president allowed me to do whatever I wanted, go wherever I chose, *carte blanche,* as the French say.

I happened to be in the Cabinet Room with Secretary of State John Hay and Secretary of War Elihu Root when TR decided to send ships to South America, creating what was called the Roosevelt corollary to the Monroe Doctrine.

"I have indicated to von Holleben that we would not intervene in their dispute with Venezuela unless they made an attempt to capture territory," Hay said. He was a white-bearded gentleman who had been a government official as far back as Lincoln. Mr. Roosevelt respected him, and Hay had the attitude of a smart, amused uncle toward TR.

"I know," TR said, after a spurt of eyeglass polishing. "He was out to see me at Sagamore. He wanted my reassurance. He left unhappy. Yesterday I had a similar conversation with the British ambassador."

TR turned to Root. "I want you to increase our presence in the Caribbean."

"What do you plan to do?" Root asked.

"Speak softly," TR said in a whisper, then suddenly raised his voice and pounded the desk. "But carry a big stick."

"Will you drag us into a war to protect a dictator who does not keep his word to the civilized powers?" Root asked.

"I am confident I can get Britain and Germany to submit the dispute to the Hague Court and let the whole matter be resolved peacefully, with dignity for all sides." TR was up and pacing.

I sat quietly in an overstuffed chair, looking up at the portrait of George Washington on the wall. I was a simple country boy in the presence of greatness.

"Brutal wrongdoing or loosening of the ties of civilized society requires intervention by some civilized nation. In the Western Hemisphere the U.S. cannot ignore this duty," the president said.

Hay nodded. Root looked like he'd heard it all before.

"Hands off our sphere of influence," Hay said.

"Exactly. Besides, I have an ulterior motive for getting our armed services ready for action." By the president's serious tone, I knew I was about to hear something of the utmost importance. Hay and Root glanced at me questioningly, but TR made it clear it was safe to talk in front of me.

It was the Panama Canal. Hay had negotiated the treaty in January, apparently with the second-in-command at the Colombian embassy. The U.S. Senate had ratified the deal in March, but the Colombian government had rebelled at the idea. The ambassador delayed signing, and then the Colombian Senate vetoed it.

"Those contemptible creatures in Bogota will not stand in the way of progress," TR said, snapping his teeth angrily. "What's good for the U.S. is good for *all* the Americas. We will get it done without dealing with the foolish and homicidal corruptionists in Bogota."

Then I heard the plan. The people of Panama were ready to rebel against Colombia. They were going to be helped along by mercenaries from the French company that stood to lose forty million dollars if the canal never got dug. As soon as the rebellion started, the president would instantly recognize Panama as an independent country, and send in Marines to support them if Colombia tried to reclaim the territory. Before the Colombians even knew what happened, we would have a deal with the spanking-new nation of Panama.

"It sounds effective," Root said, in a way that made it unclear whether he admired or despised the idea.

"You might go into the elections with a war on your hands if any of the European powers decide to intercede," Hay said.

"Public opinion may go against you," Root said. "There are some who even now criticize the Spanish-American war."

"The things that will destroy America are prosperity-at-any-price, peace-at-any-price, safety first instead of duty first, the love of soft living, and the get-rich-quick theory of life," TR said, pacing like a tiger in a cage.

It was plain to see that TR's mind was made up. Hay changed the subject. They talked about a few diplomatic matters before Hay asked, "Have you decided definitely that you will run next year?"

He shrugged and turned to me. "What do you say, Jim? Should I throw my hat, or my towel, into the ring?"

"I don't know, Mr. President, but I suspect you will."

"Why do you say that?"

"I have never seen anyone who enjoys his job as much as you. After running a country, I don't think you'd be happy doing anything else."

The three men smiled at me.

"Bully! You know me too well, James," the president said, sitting down behind his desk.

"The election is more than a year away, but I do not believe Bryan will run again," Root said. "Probably Hearst or Judge Parker will be your adversaries."

"What about the Grand Old Party?" TR asked. "They are less pleased with me than some Democrats. Will they think of challenging an incumbent?"

"Mark Hanna might make a go of it," Hay said. "But if there is anyone to watch for, it is Senator Hooke."

"Why? He's a pleasant enough chap."

"To quote the bard, he 'has a lean and hungry look, he thinks too much, such men are dangerous,'" Hay said. "I have heard he is testing the waters."

There was a knock at the door and Ike Hoover, the White House usher, stuck his head in. "General Wood, sir."

Hay and Root said their good-byes. The soldier-doctor, who was even more stern than usual, entered the Cabinet Room and said, "I must speak with you alone," giving me a look as sharp as a Bowie knife. There was more salt than pepper in his salt-and-pepper hair, but he still had the ramrod spine of the career military man.

"You may speak freely in front of Jim," TR said.

"Your left eye is permanently damaged," Wood said without fanfare.

111

I sagged into the chair. The president stroked his mustache. "You are positive?"

"The blow has caused irreparable injury, a ruptured artery. You didn't tell me how you received it but I have seen identical injuries in prize-fighters."

"John Muir injured his eye while working as a wheelwright," TR answered. "He had to rest it for a few weeks but then it was as good as new. And he had gained insight into what was worth seeing in life."

"That is not the case with you, Mr. President," Wood said. "You will not see with that eye again."

TR stared out the window for a few moments. Wood did not move. I fidgeted. The president sighed. He told Wood that there was a conspiracy afoot, and recounted the incident in which he was attacked. Already stunned by the bad news, I was shocked again when TR told Wood. But I didn't dare interrupt.

Wood looked over at me when the president was done. "You should have plotted your strategy better, rather than allowing your most valuable soldier to the front line."

"Leonard, it was *my* decision," the president said. "In Cuba, remember, even you could not keep me from leading the charge."

"You were not president then."

"Does that mean I am less a man now that I have taken the post?"

"No, but you have more responsibilities."

TR rubbed his forehead. "No one must know how I was injured. If it comes out, you will tell them that I received it in a boxing accident here. Understood?"

Wood nodded.

"Will you help me discover who is behind this?" TR asked.

"Of course," Wood said. "But remember you only have one eye left."

eleven

The bad news put a damper on my whooping it up at the scheduled reception that night, but not TR, who must have shaken hands with a thousand guests.

Hoover told me that everyone wanted to see the way the White House had been fixed up. It was nearly a year since the renovated Executive Mansion had been unveiled. Still the Roosevelts and their architects continued to modernize it. In many ways, they were making it more like it used to be, before the nineteenth-century administrations filled it with Victorian bric-a-brac. Better than a half million dollars had been spent to put up a new office building by the west side of the White House, remove the ramshackle additions, shore up the floors, enlarge the state dining room, and provide for better handling of crowds with new doorways and a porte cochere over the east side of the house.

The party began at 8:30 P.M., in the East Room. Before TR, that room had been cluttered with mismatched furnishings under a grimy frescoed ceiling, with dark wallpaper and faded carpets. Now it had polished oak floors, off-white enameled walls, marble wainscotting, three electric chandeliers—each with thirty-five hundred pieces of crystal—candelabras on marble mantels, and four bronze Roman standards.

You may wonder how I became such an architecture and interior decoration expert. It's not what you'd expect from a one-time saddle tramp who slept many a night next to his horse on the range, where the only decor was sagebrush and cactus. Audrey McFarlane was my cultural schoolmarm. I would listen to her talk just to watch her lips move, her eyes sparkle, her hair glisten.

Anyway, the crowd that night approved of the changes, though a few complained about how much it must have cost, and a couple of biddies grumbled about how much nicer it looked when Rutherford Hayes was in office. The ladies twinkled in bright-colored dresses, with all sorts of diamond and gold doodads hanging from their ears, around their necks, and on their fingers. The men looked like penguins, black and white, and bulging around the bottom where they'd been sitting too much.

All kinds of fancy ladies and gentlemen were there and I can only remember a few names. From England, there was Lord and Lady Turchin, who were very Americanized and insisted on being called Marcus and Carolyn, as well as Cecil Spring-Rice, whom TR called Springy. The rest of the British folks were real snooty and referred to the U.S. as "the colonies." From Germany, there was Baron von Holleben, who danced like he was about to topple over at any minute. I figured it was all the medals he was still sporting. He was wearing pretty much the same outfit, from white gloves to black boots, but at least he didn't have the spiked helmet on. Senator Henry Cabot Lodge was there, tall and elegant, with a clipped beard and an expression that said he was better than everyone else. There was Hay, Root, Pinchot and Wood, and a bunch of others who were introduced to me. Audrey provided a running commentary, not only on the way people were dressed, but who they were, and their backgrounds.

"Look at Francesca Fernandes there, the Spanish ambassador's wife. She's a charming lady and very much quicker on the uptake than the ambassador."

"Where is she?" I asked, looking out on a sea of faces whirling to a waltz.

"She is the one in the House of Worth ball gown."

"Which is that?" I asked.

"The ice-blue silk satin gown with woven ribbons and butterflies studded with brilliants. Her décolletage is festooned with tulle, velvet ribbon, lace, and flowers. It covers one shoulder and leaves the other bare."

"You mean the pretty, auburn-haired lady with the naked shoulder?"

She gave me a peeved glance.

"Of course, none of them are as pretty as you," I said. I watched the crowd. All I could say was that there was an awful lot of the women's anatomy showing.

I noticed TR standing stiffly on the far side of the room. I eased myself through the crowd to see what was up.

Bill Craig was right next to the president and he looked willing to knock the block off any of the three men TR was talking to. I recognized them when I got close. Unlike most of the other guests, they didn't resemble penguins—they looked like ravens, waiting for a carcass to feed on.

". . . must back off on the Northern Securities affair. Morgan said you will do irreparable harm to the country," Marcus Alonzo Hanna was saying. The big-nosed, jug-eared former senator from Ohio, and current head of the Republican Party, had the kind of face cartoonists love.

"This talk of child labor laws and a forty-hour work week—it is positively socialistic," sneered Thomas Collier Platt, New York senator. Platt, an old enemy going back to TR's days as police commissioner, moved his tall, skinny body like an unruly puppet.

"If you continue to set aside forest preserves, there will be no more wood left to finish rebuilding the Executive Mansion," Senator David Benson Hooke said in a friendly tone. At fifty years of age, the youngest of the three, he had a sincere manner and distinguished features. His strong jaw was clean-shaven, his salt-and-pepper hair perfectly in place. His gauntness seemed to say that he worked so hard, he didn't have time to eat. Unlike TR.

"I must follow my conscience," TR said.

"You will follow your conscience right out of the White House," Platt said in his quivery voice. "The Party might back Mark here, or David, next year."

Root had drifted over to the conversation. "Gentlemen," the Cabinet member said to TR's unwanted advisors. "With people like Debs and Gompers out and about stirring up the rabble, it is important that we have a president whom the rabble perceive as a populist."

Before Root plunged into a discussion with the men, he whispered to TR, "Alice is smoking in the Blue Room and causing a sensation. Again."

"I can either run the country, or control Alice," TR said. "I cannot do both and succeed at either."

"I will handle these three," Root said.

"Very well." TR sighed and was off. Craig and I trailed behind him.

Now, what happened after that is something I can be proud of, even though what I was doing at first wasn't so nice. It was my being a soreheaded fool that cracked the case wide open.

I was still jealous of Craig, and that green-eyed monster was clouding my vision. I also was letting all the royal treatment go to my head. Audrey had pointed out to me that I was talking like I was some kind of high-and-mighty politician myself. She knew how to put me in my place. But hanging around the White House rubbed off on me. I got swell-headed ideas.

To add to the problem, Mr. Roosevelt was hopped up from having his ear bent by the three ravens, and hot under the collar because of his daughter's acting up. It was not a good time to get in his way.

But I'm running ahead of myself.

In the Blue Room, Alice was seated on an upholstered blue-and-gold sofa, with young men on either side of her. They were all laughing, until the president charged in. "Jim, if you will escort these gentlemen back to the party," TR said, "I wish to have a word in private with my daughter."

"Why not let Bill do it?" I asked.

"Do as I say," Mr. Roosevelt snapped. The men were only too happy to get away. As we walked back to the East Room, I could hear TR loudly saying, "I will not have you smoking under my roof."

I sulked in the corner for a few minutes, watching the social swirl. Cabinet members and other muckety-mucks waltzed around the floor, while the Marine Band played "The Blue Danube." I saw Root dancing with the Spanish ambassador's wife. The Republican ravens had split up. Hanna was talking earnestly to Mrs. Roosevelt. Platt was boring the Turchins with a long-winded story. Hooke was talking to a bosomy blonde. She looked annoyed at his words and marched away.

"Women," Hooke said, shaking his head. "You're nothing with them, and nothing without them."

I gave him a polite smile.

"Would you like to step outside a minute for a smoke?" he asked.

"Sounds good to me."

Hooke and I walked through the Green Room to the steps of the south portico. He produced excellent Cuban cigars from a silver carrying case. Knowing that TR disliked smoking—he was enraged when cigar manufacturers used his image for an unapproved endorsement—I had avoided the habit while in his presence and around the White House. Now, the night breezes and the flavorful smoke added up to real pleasure as I stood with the senator from California.

"What is your exact relationship with the president?" he asked casually.

"I serve at his beck and call," I said unhappily. "That means putting up with Princess Alice and the smaller brats. What sort of gratitude do I get?" I regretted the sour sound of my words. Little did I know the effect they'd have on the country's future.

"He must be difficult to work for," Hooke said, testing the waters like a smart fisherman.

"I miss these things," I said, waving the cigar.

"I will have a box of them sent to you."

"Thank you, but it's hard to smoke around here. Only Alice has that privilege."

"I know the president does not like it, but I heard that he does enjoy the fruit of the grape quite a bit."

"I don't understand."

"He drinks, does he not?"

"No more than any other temperate man."

"I have heard other stories. I know several people, important people, who are very interested in what goes on in the president's household." He let the words hang in the honeysuckle-scented night air.

"What do they want to know about?" I asked.

"Does Alice have any boyfriends who are more familiar with her than a decent woman would allow?"

"Any man brave enough to get too familiar with her deserves what he gets."

"Archie and Quentin, have they ever destroyed government property, for example, desecrated the Gilbert Stuart portrait of Washington or the furniture from Lincoln? There are reports that Ted Junior is unstable owing to his father's odd behavior. Or maybe you could garner some background on Edith. We have heard she leaves the White House alone to go antique shopping. But maybe it is to meet a lover. Do you know?"

"I have not looked into it." To talk that way about the Roosevelts! But I held my tongue and my fists. An idea was taking shape.

"It might be very worthwhile to you if you did."

"How much?" I asked, trying to sound as greedy as possible.

"Ten *thousand* dollars worth, if the information is reliable and provable. You would be favorably regarded by some very, very important people."

"Who?"

He smiled mysteriously and tapped the ash from his cigar.

"Okay, what would be done with the information?"

"Perhaps we could persuade Theodore that it was in his interest, and the country's best interest, for him to avoid seeking a second term."

"Who should I pass this information to?" I asked.

"Come to my office, any time, and leave a message. I will handle it personally. We will be meeting again, I am sure. Washington is a small town when you travel in the right circles."

We shook hands. I felt like hurrying inside to wash mine, but he seemed quite pleased.

"Maybe it's best if we are not seen together," I said.

He patted my shoulder. "I admire the cut of your jib, White. You will go far."

As he headed in, I ground the remainder of the cigar he had given me under my shoe.

I could hardly wait to tell TR. But it was impossible to talk to him. He was always with someone, and I didn't want Hooke to see me whispering in TR's ear.

Hooke and Marlowe were having a chummy chat off in one corner and I wondered if I was the only Roosevelt aide to be offered thirty pieces of silver.

Alice livened up the festivities by taking TR's words literally and not smoking under his roof. The president was summoned by a Secret Service officer midway through the reception. The Secret Serviceman reported that Alice was up near the flagpole on the White House roof, enjoying a dollop of smoldering tobacco. TR sighed, then laughed, and went back to his socializing.

It was a short time later, when the president was talking to the Belgian ambassador, that I noticed a familiar figure making his way across the dance floor. Brian Patterson! I shoved through the crowd. Two Secret Servicemen grabbed me after I nearly knocked Senator Lodge into the punch bowl.

"What's all this about?" one of them asked.

"Let go, I must get to the president." I broke free, and continued my struggle. The so-called Patterson had reached TR. The Belgian ambassador had moved on, and TR and Patterson were standing inches apart.

". . . considered my offer?" Patterson was asking.

I drew my gun.

"I would accept it, if you tell me who you really are," TR said.

I went to seize Patterson, but a half-dozen Secret Servicemen, not knowing what was happening, piled on top of me. Women began screaming. Men dove under the tables. Patterson threw something on the floor. A thick cloud of smoke enveloped him. "I can get you any time, Roosevelt," I heard Patterson say.

Someone shouted "Fire!" and the crowd turned into a mob. I was on the floor, underneath four Secret Servicemen. There was pushing and shoving and fear in the air.

"Guests!" TR bellowed. "Everyone calm down! There is no need to panic. There's no fire." He stood in the middle of the room, arms raised as if to bless the whole crowd. His calm, controlled manner was like water on a flame.

The smoke began to clear and we sorted things out. Not surprisingly, the party ended early. The president seemed more amused than upset by the events.

Then I told him about Hooke.

"They mean to smear my family for low political purposes!" He gnashed his teeth like a beaver. I was glad Hooke was gone. If TR had seen him, he would have given him a fist in the snoot.

The next morning, I found the president stomping to the East Room. He was still in a bad mood.

A couple of mattresses had been laid on the floor where diplomats and bureaucrats had partied the night before. Professor Yamashita was waiting. He was no more than five feet, with a scraggly white goatee that nearly reached his chest. Wearing some sort of black dress over a white robe, he bowed deeply when the president entered.

"The professor is teaching me a type of wrestling called jiu-jitsu," Roosevelt said, removing his suit jacket.

Secretary William Loeb stuck his head in. "Mr. President, George Baer of the Reading Railroad is waiting to speak with you regarding—"

"I know what that pompous boor is here for. Let him stew in his own juices." TR stepped onto the mat and lunged at Yamashita. The professor sidestepped and tossed him, though Mr. Roosevelt outweighed the kindly Japanese man by at least a hundred pounds.

TR jumped up and charged again. This time, I could make out Yamashita lightly grasping the president's arm and guiding him in flight like he was a kite. The president landed with a thud.

"Are you okay?" I asked, rushing to where he lay.

"I am not the age or build to be whirled in the air and batted down on a mattress, but he is so skillful that I have not been hurt at all," TR said, slowly getting up.

Yamashita smiled and bowed.

TR rose, put his jacket on, and bowed to Yamashita. "But it is hardly the way for me to let off steam, being tossed about like a sack of flour."

TR met with Baer, a middle-aged mogul with the face and temper of a snapping turtle.

"It is quite canny of you and the other operators to allow this coal strike to simmer," TR accused Baer before he had a chance to even sit.

"What do you mean?"

"Strikebreakers, no bargaining in good faith, scoffing at the miners' every proposal. Waiting for the winter, so we are forced to crush the union or freeze."

"What goes on in this strike is not a matter of your concern," Baer said.

"Everything must give way to saving the people from a fearful calamity," TR said, pounding his desk. "I am forming an Anthracite Strike Commission, which will settle this matter once and for all."

"I will fight you on this. The other mine operators are with me. You cannot meddle in private affairs," Baer said.

"Who else will represent the worker against the giant combine?"

"You listen to me, Roosevelt. The election is one year away. I'm not alone in saying that we will fight you with every resource we have. I will give up my fortune to see you defeated."

"The panel will be composed of respected gentlemen who will render a fair and just decision," TR said, ignoring Baer's bluster. "I am acting in the miners' interest, in the nation's interest, and ultimately, in your own interest. Good day, Mr. Baer."

Like the angry turtle he resembled, Baer snapped, buried his head in his shoulders, and slowly walked out. I told TR what Baer reminded me of. He grinned, but he was bubbling like a geyser about to explode.

He changed into casual clothes, and hurried to the tennis court, which was just outside the office wing. Since I did not play the game, he summoned Assistant Secretary of State Lindsay Cheney, and went at it. He held the racket midway up the stem, and smashed the ball with ferocity. After an hour of play he was covered with a sheen of sweat, but appeared calmer. He had beaten Cheney, who was a half-dozen years younger and had sixty pounds less weight to carry around the court.

"I have decided," the president said, as a White House aide scurried over with a fresh towel. He wiped his face vigorously. "I will go to Massachusetts to test the waters. I know the Republican political leaders oppose me, as of course do the Democrats. The combines will have millions to spend against me. I must get an indication of how the people feel."

He said Massachusetts had big cities and small towns he could gauge the sentiments of. Unlike New York and Washington, he did not have a long, well-known history of public service in the Commonwealth. I tried to convince him not to, that we should stay in Washington and concentrate on Senator Hooke. But I couldn't sway him and finally gave in. "When do we leave?"

"Not we. You must stay here. Be my eyes and ears. When the cat is away, the rats will play. You must sniff out as much as you can. I will only be gone a few days."

I suppose, in a way, it was fortunate I didn't go with him. If I had, I might have suffered the same fate as poor Bill Craig.

twelve

My digging hit a few dry holes. I snooped around the apartment where Maude Adams—or whatever her name was—got killed. I got in by pretending to be a police officer. But the apartment held no clues.

I spent hours outside both the Colombian and German delegations, to see if any of the muscle men we had bumped heads with showed up. The long surveillances gave me nothing but a runny nose and a chill.

Thanks to Hooke, I did get to meet a robber baron I had heard a lot about—Ronald Crittenden. It was at a reception at the German embassy, with Baron von Holleben the host. In the ballroom, ladies and gentlemen in finery waltzed. The baron was in top form, clicking his heels together constantly and kissing the ladies' hands. His medals clinked like sleigh bells.

Crittenden looked like Saint Nicholas with a trimmed beard. He had rosy red cheeks and an ample girth. If he had been dressed in red, instead of a black tuxedo, I think mothers would have been tempted to put their toddlers on his lap. He greeted me like we were old friends.

"Senator Hooke speaks highly of you," Crittenden said.

"He's too kind," I forced myself to say.

"He said you are, how should I say it, ah, disillusioned with Mr. Roosevelt?"

"That's safe to say. He doesn't know how to treat people fair."

"I am involved with a—how should I put it—a coalition of businessmen, politicians, prominent leaders, who want to make sure the right person is in the White House in 1905."

"Someone like Senator Hooke."

"Precisely."

"I will help any way I can," I said. "Who else is loyal to the cause?"

The Santa Claus eyes stopped twinkling and I instantly realized I had made a mistake. Crittenden was neither fanatic nor fool.

"I need to know who I can trust," I said, trying to explain.

"Trust no one," he said in a monotone. "You already know the senator. Deal through him. Excuse me." He spotted a Maryland congressman, buttonholed him, and got into a deep conversation.

I socialized for a while more with several elegantly coiffed ladies trying to find out who I was, what I was doing there, and if I was available. None of them could hold a candle to Audrey. I made small talk, keeping my answers vague, though I let them know I was an important man at the White House. I later saw one of the more persistent women in a corner whispering to Crittenden.

During a stint as a hotel detective in St. Louis, I had developed the knack of spotting women-of-the-night. It's not as easy as you think if it's the higher-priced ladies and not the common street-walkers. The judgment had to be based on clothing, makeup, and manner. Long eye contact, through droopy bedroom eyes, was a sure giveaway. There was no question that several of the ladies at Holleben's party were not ladies.

As the night wore on there were fewer couples or people I had seen at the White House. More and more it was single men and trollops. The waltzing stopped, and the musicians played popular tunes like "Ida, Sweet as Apple Cider," "The Belle of Avenue A," and "I Wonder Who's Kissing Her Now." The gas lamps were dimmed and the dancers held each other indecently close. Hooke was cheek to cheek with a woman who could have been no more than half his fifty years. I was approached many times by women who asked me to dance. Waiters circulated, practically forcing potent drinks down guests' throats. I nursed one for an hour. I had to keep my wits about me.

It was almost midnight when I found myself next to Hooke.

"A fantashtic party, ishn't it?" he slurred.

"Very nice," I said. "So many familiar faces."

"Yesh."

"Isn't that Congressman Slayden?" I asked, pointing to one gentleman with his hand on a young blonde's fanny.

"No. Thash Mudge. He's in coal and lumber. Salt-of-the-earth fellow."

Continuing to act cagey, I duped him into identifying several of the guests.

"Looksh like we might not be needing your information anyway," Hooke said, swaying slightly as he leaned against the large grandfather clock.

"Really. Why not?" I asked casually.

"With any luck, the Roosevelt problem is being taken care of even as we speak."

"How's that?"

He burped and took a sip from his glass. The pendulum on the clock next to us swung back and forth. Tick, tock, tick, tock. I wished I could have grabbed him and shaken the information out.

"Accidents will happen," Hooke muttered to himself.

Crittenden rushed over. "Senator, Jim, you are not enjoying the party. You must get out and mingle."

"Mingle, jingle, bingle, single," Hooke said.

"Senator, there is a pretty lady who has been asking about you all night."

"Really?"

Crittenden snapped his fingers and a woman with rouged cheeks and blond hair tied with a red ribbon came over and took Hooke's arm. "You're such a handsome man," she cooed, leading him away.

"What was he saying to you?"

I tried to sound as drunk as Hooke had been. "Something about Roosevelt and accidents. I guessh he was talking about McKinley getting shot or something. Would you join me for a drink?"

"Another time," he said, scrutinizing me closely.

I angled toward the door, moving as fast as I could without getting anyone suspicious. The two dozen partygoers still at it were dancing to ragtime music.

Crittenden was watching me. I spotted a plump drunken tart clinging to a potted plant for support. "Can I have this dance?" I asked, taking her in my arms before she could answer.

"Better look out, sailor," she said, and hiccuped. "Candy doesn't feel too good."

"But you look so wonderful." Her skin was deathly pale wherever it was not covered by layers of makeup. With my face near hers, I was surrounded by the smell of liquor and perfume. But I kept her moving toward the door.

"Not so fast," she told me. "I ain't a racehorse, you know. I'm going to be sick."

We were right near the door. "Let's go outside."

Crittenden appeared like an unwelcome spirit. "Where are you going?" he demanded.

"Candy ish sick," I said with my arms still around her. Her flesh felt soft, unhealthy, like there were no bones under her tight-fitting bodice. "I planned to take her outshide for some air.

Then maybe I'll take her home." I gave him a broad leer and a wink.

"Is that true?" he asked her.

She looked up, her face now a bluish white. "I don't know. He—"

Crittenden couldn't see, but she could definitely feel, as I suddenly pressed her stomach. She gagged.

"Get her out of here," Crittenden barked.

"I was trying," I said, and hustled her out. I gave her my handkerchief when she was done. She wiped her mouth, and then tried to hit me.

"You caused that you sonofabitch. Now I'll never get invited back."

"How much do you make for one of these nights?"

"What do you mean?"

"I know what you are, what the other women there were. How much do you get?"

"Twenty dollars, if we land a good one."

"What's your name. Your real name?" I said, taking a double-eagle gold piece out of my pocket, tossing it in the air, and catching it.

"Griselda. Griselda Guerney."

"Where do you live?"

"Fourteenth and H. Would you like to come back with me?"

"Let me call you a cab. But I might be in touch sometime soon. I want a favor from you."

"I specialize in favors."

"If anyone asks, I came back with you to your flat tonight."

"Yeah?"

I tossed her the coin.

She smiled. "For this, I'll tell anyone who asks you were a real stud horse."

I put her in a hansom a few blocks away at Dupont Circle and raced back to the White House as soon as she was out of sight. With the aid of that remarkable gadget, the telephone, I was confident I could warn TR in time. I rushed past the White House police, nearly getting shot by an overanxious guard.

As my feet pounded on the entrance hall floor, I knew right away something was wrong. Lights were burning and the staff was moving about even though it was well after midnight. I found Audrey on her way to the south end of the Executive Mansion holding a small china tray with teapot and crackers.

"What happened?" I asked.

She stared at me and sniffed like a trained bloodhound. "A trolley struck the president's carriage," she said coldly, and strode away.

I followed at her heels. "Is he okay?"

"Your concern is appreciated. Did you have a good time tonight?"

"Damn it, woman, I will explain later. How is he?"

"Mr. Roosevelt suffered bruises to his head and face. His leg is broken. It might have to be amputated. Bill Craig was not as fortunate."

"Not as fortunate?"

"No. He is dead."

thirteen

Mrs. Roosevelt was sitting at a table in the Blue Room, as if waiting for her Tuesday morning embroidery group. "Thank you, Audrey," she said, as the maid poured her tea. "How are you, Mr. White?"

"I am fine, Mrs. Roosevelt. I heard the tragic news just now."

"Poor Mr. Craig. Such a fine young man. He was Theodore's favorite. And the boys' as well." She sipped the tea. Behind her hung the portrait by Theobold Chartran, a gift from France to the United States. The painting showed Edith Roosevelt seated on a white bench in front of the south portico. She held white gloves and an ebony parasol. She looked relaxed but elegant. The canvas seemed to have more life than the subject sitting before it.

A sleepy-eyed Alice came in. "Are you all right, Mother?"

Mrs. R nodded. For once quiet, Alice sat next to her mother, and looked at me with mature eyes.

There was a skittering sound on the stairway. Archie and Quentin came running in, pursued by a governess. "I tried to stop them, but . . ." the panting nursemaid began.

The children bounded to Mrs. Roosevelt, who waved at the governess to show it was okay. Then Kermit, looking even more absent-minded with sleep clouding his face, and a sad-faced Ethel entered. They all huddled around their mother. "Don't worry, Mother. Nothing can hurt Daddy," Quentin said.

My eyes met hers. Her lids fluttered as if she had momentarily lost control, but she kept her emotions in check.

Audrey and I left the Roosevelt family and shut the big wooden door on the way out.

"Just where were you?" she asked, as we stood near the stairs to the second floor.

"At a reception."

"You stink of liquor and perfume and God only knows what else," she said. "It must have been quite an affair."

"I was working for the president."

"I am sure he appreciates that as he lies in a hospital bed in Boston. Mr. Craig would too, if he were alive."

"I feel bad enough as it is. There's no need to make me feel worse. I was working," I said. "I picked up valuable information."

"Such as?"

"It's for the president's ears only. You must understand."

"I understand your shenanigans perfectly," she said, and marched away. I started to call out to her, but knew it would be useless unless I told her everything.

Dr. Wood, who had rushed up to Boston, telephoned us early the next morning with the news that Mr. Roosevelt was in stable condition. The wound on his leg was showing signs of infection. Amputation was being considered to prevent deadly gangrene.

I got the news from a stone-faced Audrey McFarlane. I felt terrible about what had happened, and worse about myself. I had let Mr. Roosevelt down and now he lay at death's door. The target of my silly jealousy had died in service to his country. Audrey hated me. I was no good to anyone.

By 10 A.M. I was over on Fourteenth Street. I made my way up and down that street of honky-tonks, rowdy saloons, and clip joints. I sampled every cheap burlesque and vaudeville house, in between downing flagons of beer and bourbon. I wound up spending that night at Griselda's, which cost me plenty financially—and in self-respect. I rapidly ran through my money, pouring grog down my gullet. My barroom buddies did not understand why I was so busted up over the president's accident.

"He's better off'n McKinley," one buddy said.

"That Rosenfelt's one of them rich bastards don't give a tinker's dam about us," a shabby man with a red nose said. "He was born rich, he lives rich, he's gonna die rich."

"But he cares about regular folks," I said. "He's for all Americans. He wants a square deal and a decent life for everybody."

"He's a fat hypocrite," another man piped up. "He talks about saving nature, but every time I see something about him, he's on a hunting trip somewhere."

"It's true he likes to hunt, but he's set aside millions of acres for park land for all of us to enjoy. Some of the most beautiful spots in the country."

We argued back and forth, me defending the president against a slew of bitter drunks. I had enough presence of mind left not to reveal the conspiracy. Not that my fellow souses would have believed me. By my third day on the binge, I was with tipplers who thought they were Kaiser Wilhelm, Napoleon, and Ulysses S. Grant.

In the back room of one bar, the People's Tavern, I stumbled into a meeting of radicals. They ranted and raved about the evils of big business and its cohort, the government. A mushy-featured fellow with a knife-sharp widow's peak hopped on a chair. "I only regret the trolley did not kill Roosevelt," the speaker said. "He is nothing but a patsy for big business, a front man who allows the Rockefellers to get rich while the honest workingman can't feed his wife and children."

He kept talking about starving workers, but he himself must

have tipped the scale at three hundred pounds. The chair under him creaked every time he moved. He told lies about the First Family, saying Edith wasted millions on fancy decoration for herself, while Alice used tax money to buy a new dress every day. He said TR was a drunken madman who kept horses in the White House and laughed when his children whipped the staff. He said the whole family should be taken out and executed, the way the French people cleared out their tyrants.

I tried to stand and defend the president, but I was too drunk. I rose and promptly fell back into my seat. I awoke to find the bartender shaking my shoulder. The tavern was closing. Griselda was not at home or on her street corner, and I wound up sleeping on a park bench.

I was at a seedier bar the next day when the door crashed open and in stormed a woman nearly six feet tall, with a fanatic gleam in her eye, and an axe in her hand. She was homely and big and mean. I thought she was a predecessor of the pink elephants. But the sound of her axe as it crashed into the bar near my head did wonders for clearing my noggin. The axe-wielding madwoman was helped by two others with crowbars, who smashed tables, bottles, and the long oak bar. I huddled under a table, joined by another drunk looking for shelter.

"We being invaded?" I asked.

"It's the Women's Christian Temperance Union! *That* is Carrie Nation."

"Who?"

"The woman from Kansas who wants to make the country dry."

"Why I never—"

An axe thumped into the table above us and we were silent. Then I heard police whistles. The bartender was struggling with one of the women who was trying to smash the mirror behind the bar. A man who had been struck by flying glass was bleeding and cursing. Nation screamed about "the evil demon rum."

As the police charged in, I crawled out, finding my way to a back door. I was in an alleyway. A scrawny gray cat stood atop the garbage pile and hissed at me. The garbage looked so comfortable, I staggered over to it, and went to sleep.

A stick poked me. I tried to knock it away, but it was persistent. I opened one eye. It was General Wood, as stone-faced as the coldest statue. I tried to get to my feet, but fell backwards.

"I was—"

"Shut up. You are a disgrace. Can you walk?"

"Yes, sir."

"Good. I want you at the rear entrance of the State, War and Navy Building in a half hour. Think you can handle that?"

"Yes, sir. But how did you find me?"

"The president has been asking for you since we got back. He has everyone out scouring the city. I guessed that you would sink to this level."

"But I—"

"I am not interested in excuses. You will report to the building so I can get you cleaned up. I'm afraid if the president saw you he would be heartsick."

"How is he?"

But Wood was already striding off.

Somehow I managed to get to my feet. No hansom driver would pick me up and a trolley-car conductor refused to let me on, so I dragged my body, step by step, down Fourteenth and over onto Vermont. I made it in time.

The four-story State, War and Navy Building was a commanding sight, with its purple-gray exterior and nine hundred free-standing columns. Copper mansard roofs and chimneys topped the massive structure. Wood was waiting on the back steps. He led me to an office on the first floor, then through a door to a private bathroom.

"Clean up," he barked.

I shaved, showered, and changed into an outfit he had smuggled from the White House. I gulped four cups of steaming black coffee.

"What should I do with this?" I asked, pointing to my heap of clothing. I had found a pair of woman's garters in my pocket, but was able to hide that from him.

"I shall have it burned," he said, nudging the pile with his riding crop.

fourteen

I had never seen Theodore Roosevelt looking pale and weak, so the sight that greeted me in his bedroom hit me like a blow from a bullwhip.

He sat in an oversized wing chair, leg extended and resting on a red velvet ottoman. Mrs. Roosevelt sat on a matching chair with a mailbag at her feet. She was reading a letter. TR was also reading. He held a copy of Sun Tzu's *The Art of War* in his hand. On his lap were books by Tacitus and Herodotus.

"How are you, Mr. President?"

He managed a smile. "I doubt if I will be up to teaching you tennis today. Where have you been?"

"Looking into things. I was working at getting contacts in the underworld here."

"I assumed you were some place disreputable. Leonard would not tell me where he found you, but his mustache was curled up tight with displeasure."

"I have news, but it would be better if you and I discussed it privately. With all due respect to Mrs. Roosevelt."

"I have told Edie everything," TR said, patting his wife's hand affectionately. "She is too formidable an ally, or adversary, to ignore."

So I told them about my night at the German embassy with Crittenden and Hooke, and a considerably bowdlerized version of my recent days and nights in the Washington underworld.

TR stroked his mustache.

"We can have Crittenden and Hooke arrested immediately," I said.

Mrs. Roosevelt shook her head. "I think not. It is like Theodore's infection. All the disease in the limb must be removed before the body can be truly healthy."

"Bully!" he said, squeezing her hand. "Who needs Machiavelli when I have the best counselor in the world."

"How many people knew your exact route beforehand?" I asked.

"To arrange this 'accident'," he said, touching his bandaged leg, "required an individual closer to me than I had suspected."

"Who did know, Mr. President?"

"Aside from myself and Edith, Bill Craig, John Hay, Elihu Root, and Marlowe."

"I would wager it's Marlowe," I said.

"That's quite an accusation to make about a member of the Secret Service," TR said. "Are you sure?"

"I for one would not be surprised," Edith said. "I never had a good feeling about that man."

"Women's intuition," he said with a chuckle. "Have you anything more substantive before we hang him for treason?" he asked me.

"I saw him and Senator Hooke jawing like old bunkhouse mates."

"That is far from enough to put a rope around his neck, but it does move him to the top of the list of suspects."

"It is unpleasant for me to say this, Theodore, but if a conspiracy exists, it is possible that others on the list might also be involved," Mrs. R said.

He suddenly looked very, very tired.

"Should I come back later?" I asked.

"Perhaps you could go and get General Wood. There is a matter I'd like to discuss with both of you."

I raced to the State, War and Navy Building. The general was in Elihu Root's office. I found the two men discussing the Philippines.

"The president would like to see you," I told Wood.

"How is his health?" Root asked.

"As well as can be expected," I said.

"He is as strong as he is obstinate," Root said.

I regarded him suspiciously. Did his talking against TR mean he was part of the conspiracy? Who could be trusted?

Wood and I hurried back to the Executive Mansion.

TR had renewed his strength, and Edith was reading a letter to him from a well-wisher in New Jersey.

"We have received more than a thousand letters," TR said. "I will make sure that every last one is answered. The children are writing responses at this very moment."

Wood walked over and felt Theodore's head. "Your fever is up."

"I am burning with anger and frustration. I have a plan, however, and will need your assistance."

Wood nodded, taking TR's wrist and checking his pulse.

"I want the word spread that I am in top shape. Whatever it takes to make me fit for public appearances must be done. There can be no sign of weakness or else these jackals will close in."

"There is a drug that can help. It's called cocaine."

"I've read of it. An alkaloid derived from the coca leaf. A central-nervous-system stimulant with anaesthetic properties."

"It also can cause hallucinations and delusions of persecution," Wood said. "The drug is not one to be given out willy-nilly. Prescribing it includes serious risks. But it will ease the pain and keep you on your feet."

"Fine," he said. There was the hint of a shudder.

"Just relax and be still. I want to examine that wound," Wood said. Even the tough soldier was moved by TR's refusal to accept the pain. He knelt before the president like a knight before a king and began undoing the bandages.

"Edith, perhaps you should see how the children are doing," TR suggested. She squeezed his hand and left.

It was an ugly gash stretching below his knee to mid-shin. I smelled the stink of diseased flesh.

"Not good," Wood muttered. "I must operate again."

"So be it," TR said. "There is one matter which must be attended to before you sharpen your scalpel."

"Yes?"

"There aren't many I trust in the Secret Service and White House police. I need men I can have absolute faith in. I want these men." TR handed Wood a list of a dozen names.

"Don Ray, Bob Ferguson, Schuyler Sprowles, and these others. The names are familiar."

"Rough Riders," I said with a grin.

"The cream of the crop," TR said. "Jim can help determine the best way to deploy them. I would like two men to be assigned to keep an eye on young Ted at Groton. I suggest Sprowles and Ferguson. They can best blend in to the hallowed halls of academe. Some of the others would wind up assaulting the dean." He gritted his teeth and shuddered. "I had better get back to my reading," he said, picking up a book. Like a great beast, he wanted to be alone in his suffering.

"We must get you to a hospital," Wood said that night, after the president's temperature climbed to 104 degrees and his body shook with violent tremors.

"Whatever needs to be done can be done here," TR said.

"There is no way this room could be sterilized sufficiently for me to attempt surgery," Wood said.

"The White House is far more sterile than the field hospitals in Cuba where so many valiant men were treated for shrapnel and Mauser rounds," TR said in a wobbly voice. "I cannot risk word of my condition leaking out. You must perform the necessary treatment here."

The general was no more successful in changing TR's mind than I ever was. The surgery was conducted in the study with Alice and me assisting Dr. Wood. The president's daughter showed the kind of spunk he would have been proud of, calmly handing Dr. Wood the proper instruments as he made a two-inch cut and scraped clean the bone.

After the operation, Wood gave Alice a peck on the cheek, and firmly shook my hand. "You both have my grateful thanks." He marched out before we could say anything.

I smiled at Alice. "You are a very brave young lady."

"Thank you. I must go," she said, and ran from the room with a sick expression on her face. I was left alone with the unconscious president.

He was as helpless as a babe, his face and body relaxed across the hard metal table we had wheeled in to perform the operation on. I had scrubbed it three times with carbolic acid before TR lay on it. His breathing was labored.

I watched his chest rise and fall, and prayed.

The next day, he was behind the huge desk—made from the timbers of the British ship *Resolute* —in his study on the second floor. His crutches were hidden in a closet. Only the members of the family, myself, Secretary Loeb, and Dr. Wood knew his true condition. We worked to take as much of the burden off Mr. Roosevelt as was possible.

Mrs. Roosevelt was able to handle many of his social functions alone. Alice and Ethel enjoyed playing nurse. Whenever a meeting was going on too long, Edith would loose "the dogs of war" and Archie and Quentin would attack, disrupting long-winded ambassadors, tenacious lobbyists, pompous senators, and unwelcome bureaucrats. Usually a few war whoops or mock Rough Rider charges by the boys were enough to convince any visitor his meeting was over. But Quentin had to produce a slimy frog to get the ladies from the Woman's Christian Temperance Union to skedaddle. Carrie Nation was not with them or the little critter would have been whacked with an axe.

Crittenden was one of his callers. The jovial Santa Claus looked like he had aged ten years in the short time since I'd last seen him. "Have you ever assigned a task and found your servant has far exceeded your command?" the robber baron asked TR.

"I don't have time for hypothetical questions," the president said.

"Sometimes a man starts something rolling, and it takes off out of control," Crittenden said. He waited for TR to respond. The president removed his glasses and gave them a slow buffing. Crittenden squirmed.

"I have always taken responsibility for my actions, as well as the actions of those under my command, whether it be in Cuba, Sagamore Hill, or the White House," TR finally said.

Crittenden buried his face in his hands. "I suspect it has gone too far," he said, talking to himself. "I didn't realize how much he had on me, what he planned to do."

"Who's 'he'?" I asked.

Crittenden stood up. "I shouldn't have come here," he said to

TR. "I have never begged in my life. I will not start now. Good-bye." He marched from the room.

"Should I bring him back?" I asked the president.

"It wouldn't do any good. He wanted to make a deal. He's started an avalanche, and hopes to stop it with a shovel," TR said. "We cannot question him without tipping off the others."

"Maybe we could—"

"If I allow him to weasel out from under this, he will only try again. I know his type. This conspiracy must be crushed resoundingly. I cannot show an individual mercy at the risk of jeopardizing an entire nation."

That same day, I was walking around the grounds, a habit I had picked up for purposes of exercise as well as security, when I heard a fuss at the front gate. A half dozen White House police were wrestling with a man, and getting the worst of it. Two guards had drawn their guns, but could not fire for fear of hitting their fellow officers.

I ran over to help just as the intruder shrugged off the last couple of guards. I was face-to-face with a five-foot four-inch terror. "Don't shoot," I told the guards.

"Jimmy, you old so and so," the intruder said.

"Spider Monaghan, you little cuss. You could've gotten yourself killed."

"If they did that, then I'd a known they was good enough to guard Colonel Roosevelt. I mean, the president."

And so it was that the Rough Riders rode into town. Not all of them made as slam-bang an entrance as Monaghan, but word was soon out that something was going on. We passed it off as a mini-reunion, planning for a bigger one that would be scheduled next year. The reporters swallowed the story, figuring that TR would love to see a get-together right before the election to remind voters of his heroism in the Spanish-American war.

Seeing the old boys, as full of energy as Archie and Quentin, was tonic for Mr. Roosevelt. And knowing that men he could trust with his life were watching out for him and his family aided in his recovery.

We didn't tell the Rough Riders exactly what was going on, only that TR needed them for extra security. They took to the job with pleasure.

Another new recruit, while not a former Rough Rider, had heard through the grapevine that TR was looking for men who could handle themselves. This recruit definitely could. He had been thrown out of several towns for handling himself too well. His name was Bartholomew Masterson, but everyone called him Bat. I had shared a few drinks with him once in Colorado. He was a droopy-eyed, droopy-mustached gent who had a reputation for being fair but a bit too quick on the trigger. His taste for gambling and liquor made him not very popular in towns as they sought respectability. TR and I enjoyed having him around and listening to stories about Dull Knife's Cheyenne tribe, Doc Holliday, Dodge City, Tombstone, and the Earp brothers.

TR went back to his usual schedule, rising at 7:30 A.M. to exercise and joining the family for breakfast by 8:15. After as much as half an hour spent walking—or more accurately, limping—with his wife, TR would go to the West Wing and attack paperwork with Loeb's help.

That week he began toting a full work load again. He fired off a letter to the Kaiser telling him that Baron von Holleben was not serving Germany's interests in Washington. He sent a thank-you note responding to a get-well message from King Edward VII of Great Britain. He hinted at the trouble in Venezuela, and assured them the United States did not want war—or European interference—in Latin America. He created the Public Lands Commission to study the use of undeveloped land and work closely with local governments. The commission, sparked by Pinchot and Muir, was to make sure political cronies didn't get mineral rights and such through pork-barrel legislation. The president also met with Oliver Wendell Holmes, his Supreme Court appointee, to discuss a recent vacancy in the High Court.

I lost track of all the important men who visited him in those busy days—but I know they included Hay, Root, and a couple of dozen senators. Among them was Hooke, whom TR welcomed particularly vigorously. Hooke signaled that he wished to talk, and I arranged to be near the doorway when he exited.

"How is the president?" he asked.

"As healthy as a horse."

"Is he taking any drugs? Any sign of infections, complications?"

"None that I know of. He's talking about playing tennis again soon."

Hooke bit his lip.

Of course I reported the conversation to TR at lunchtime. That was when the strain of handling presidential business would show, behind closed doors, when he would collapse into a chair and Wood would have to give him another injection of cocaine.

TR made few concessions to his health, despite lobbying by Edith, Dr. Wood, and myself. Probably the toughest job was dealing with the dozens of newsmen, who invariably wanted to know about his injury. TR would laugh and dismiss it as a "bad scratch."

The revolution began in Panama with American troops conveniently nearby. Our Marines landed at Colon and prevented the Colombian army from getting into Panama. TR announced that the United States was recognizing Panama as a sovereign nation, their newly appointed ambassador hurried to the White House, and by day's end we had a treaty for the Panama Canal on terms satisfactory to TR.

Relations between myself and Audrey McFarlane remained as strained as those between the United States and Colombia. I was frustrated that I could not tell her the truth, and riled that she was so quick to give me the cold shoulder. After more than a week of ignoring each other, on a Sunday afternoon, she ran up and put her arms around me.

"I have heard the whole story," she said. "I am so, so sorry."

"What whole story?"

"About your undercover work for the president. You are as wonderful as I thought."

My first reaction was joy at our peace treaty. Then I realized what it meant. I questioned her thoroughly. She had heard that I was acting as the president's confidential investigator, trying to get to the bottom of some sort of conspiracy against him.

"Where did you hear that?" I asked.

"From Ike Hoover."

I rushed to the White House usher, who told me he had heard it from one of the cooks. I ran from one end of the White House to the other, trying to find the original blabbermouth. No dice. At least a half dozen people knew of my role. Audrey guessed that it must have gotten out when one of the servants overheard a conversation they shouldn't have.

The next day, the scandal sheets reported the president being as ill as McKinley was right before he died. Rumors were spreading fast.

TR did not have a vice-president, so Daniel Creange, the president pro tem of the Senate, was next in line. He was pounced on by yellow journalists and asked if it was true he had been told not to leave Washington. Creange brushed the pests off, saying Roosevelt was healthy enough to be president for fifty more years.

The president called the press together for a conference. He moved briskly about the room on his cane as he told them he was fit as a fiddle. But the more perceptive reporters could see it wasn't true. Fortunately, they did not see him after the fifteen-minute session, when he sagged into a chair in the West Wing and suffered a frightening asthma attack.

Reporters swarmed around Surgeon General Rixey and General Wood. Both men fended them off, with Wood storming away after one member of the fourth estate asked if TR had prepared a will. I personally had to restrain one of the Rough Riders who caught a reporter asking Quentin if he was scared his daddy was going to die. While I was holding the Wyoming cowboy, Quentin kicked the reporter in the shins.

Back in the White House, TR roared with laughter when he heard of the incident. But the fact that his family was being badgered disturbed him more than anything. "The press will only believe what they see with their own eyes," TR said. "There is only one solution."

"What?" Wood, Loeb, Edith, the children, and myself asked simultaneously.

"A point-to-point."

"No!" we all said.

For those of you who have never had the pleasure, Rock Creek Park has more than seventeen hundred acres of land following the course of Rock Creek through northwest Washington. The President loved to go riding there with Mrs. R and to take the members of his tennis cabinet for brisk hikes through tree-lined gullies, hills, and ravines.

We stood outside Fort De Russy near Oregon Avenue and Military Road. The president leaned on a cane. Besides myself, there was Alice, General Wood, four of our Rough Riding buddies, Gifford Pinchot, and two dozen reporters.

"Much has been written in the past days about how Theodore Roosevelt will not be around to see the morning sun. This came as quite a shock to me. While I suffered a minor accident, the newspapers were preparing my obituary. This may be a long-standing practice in your business, but it is considered good form to avoid running it until the subject is no longer breathing."

A few reporters chuckled. Most were squinting at the president, looking for signs of weakness. TR leaned heavily on a stout cane, but he appeared robust.

Not so the reporters. There were broken blood vessels on noses, stooped shoulders, nicotine-stained fingers, beery bellies. I doubted if many of them had been up this early in years. Some of them had probably not yet been to bed, having come to the park right from receptions. Most were in their thirties. Very few were as old as the president.

"To believe what many of you have written, I am mortally injured and ready to make my peace," TR was saying. "So the least you can do is keep up as I hobble through the park. At the end, those who survive will be rewarded with a good story. You know the rules. Let us be off then."

So began a trek that became a legend in Washington journalism circles. The Rough Riders and I scanned the bushes, keeping an eye out for potential assassins. The other members of the president's party kept the herd moving.

The only rule in a point-to-point is that the group must follow the leader on a straight line, whether that means walking over rocks, roofs, or rivers. When journalists began falling behind, Pinchot needled them along. He would seize their arms and drag them, lecturing on trees and complaining about wasting good wood pulp on scurrilous lies. The general made use of his riding crop on more than a few posteriors. Alice employed feminine wiles, and many a flirtatious young reporter pushed himself harder than he thought possible to keep up with the flounce of her skirt.

At the end of three miles, I was breathing hard. Five reporters turned back.

We scaled cliffs, plunged into the ice-cold creek in its widest spots, climbed over boulders, and fought with branches. By the five-mile mark, another dozen had fallen. Even Pinchot had stopped rhapsodizing about the beauty of nature.

Wood would hurry to catch up with TR when they could be on the other side of a hill and out of view of the pack of pundits. Once I was close enough to hear the general ask, "Do you need any more? How are you holding up?"

"Dee-lightful," TR responded, loud enough to frighten birds from their trees. He had a few scratches on his face from whiplike branches, sweat was dripping from his brow, and his eyes had a peculiar glaze behind his glasses.

We came to a waterfall that had all but dried up. But the rocks left behind by the water were smooth as a frog's belly and just as slippery. I still don't know how TR made it over them, but he did, and at a pace that amazed me. It was the final straw for several reporters, who tumbled between rocks, yelping as they found themselves in a cold brook or on tufts of slimy moss. Many an ankle was sprained and I wouldn't even guess how many pants were torn.

Three reporters finished the ten-mile hike with us.

"I promised you gentlemen a story and I shall make good on my word. Shortly before our little constitutional I received word that I have been selected to be the umpire of claims in the dispute between Germany, Great Britain, and Venezuela. I look forward to making an amicable peace and just settlement for all nations concerned," TR said slowly, allowing himself a deep breath between each sentence. "Do any of you have any questions?"

"Guh—guh—guh—" the reporters gasped.

"I should like to congratulate you," he said. "Anything worth achieving requires labor, effort, serious purpose, and willingness to run risks. This is true for the individual, as well as the nation. If there are no further questions, I bid you good day, gentlemen. You might want to alert the editors of the other papers to have someone retrieve your fallen colleagues."

Two closed carriages were waiting. I got into the first one with TR, Alice, and General Wood. "That cocaine is an amazing drug," the general said. "I think I would do a paper on its efficacy if I could talk about this case."

"Leonard, I have not taken any of that powder you gave me for the past two days," the president said.

Then Mr. Roosevelt's eyes rolled up and he passed out.

fifteen

Thanks to Wood's care and the sturdy Roosevelt physique, the president was soon back on his feet. Well, not exactly back, for he still tried to conduct the affairs of state while seated.

He would meet with his advisors in the Cabinet room, mentally juggling business affecting the Departments of the Treasury, Navy, Interior, and Agriculture. He had particularly tough questions for Attorney General Philander Knox, who was running the Northern Securities case.

TR saved his latter hours for Root and Hay, whom he respected most. Sometimes TR asked Hay, who had started his government career as a secretary under Lincoln, how he thought the Great Emancipator would have handled this or that crisis.

TR always said he believed in a Jackson–Lincoln theory of the presidency. He explained that, "When a national crisis arises which calls for immediate, vigorous executive action, it's the president's duty to do what's needed, unless the Constitution or the laws explicitly forbid it."

He would have arguments with Hay and Root over what that meant. Sometimes Senator Henry Cabot Lodge would join them, usually siding with TR. I would sit like a bump on a log, knowing

I was listening to the great minds of our time, and being smart enough to keep my trap shut.

With his family, he was helping the tutor prepare Kermit for Groton; romping with his two youngest, which he termed the best exercise of all; playing hide-and-seek with Ethel; writing Teddy at school; being a loyal and loving husband to his wife; and trying to keep Alice out of trouble. Even on a slow day, more things happened with them than under the big top in a Ringling Brothers Circus.

Arthur Brown at last came to the White House with answers to the questions TR had asked him in that New York pub: Zach, Grace, and the man with the tattoos, whose name was Daley, were part of a repertory company that toured the United States.

"They go under the name—now let me get this right—the Amazing Amusements and Mystifying Performances Repertory Company and Road Show, Limited," Brown said, reading from his small notebook.

They had moved from the Grand Opera House in Brooklyn, to a theater in Hartford, and then Boston. The trio were former carnival workers, who had a dozen arrests between them for disturbing the peace, assault, or fraud.

"When were they in Boston?" TR asked.

"Let me see, let me see, ah, they began there a month ago and left two weeks ago."

"Interesting," TR said. "Do go on."

"Raoul Aguilar was a ponce. Marla was one of several women he used."

"Did he have any connections with this repertory company?" TR asked.

"None that I could find," Brown said. "The most valuable item, however, is not the information. It is this," he continued, and with a flourish, he withdrew a yellowed and faded photograph from his pocket. "At great risk, and through methods so devious I outdid myself, I secured this, the only known picture of the man known as Spike," Brown said. "It was taken seven years ago, right after he shot a saloon keeper who failed to make payments to his gang. Since then he has risen greatly in stature in the underworld. He can be enjoying a meal at the Waldorf while his enemies are being slaughtered by his army of strong-arms." Brown passed over the photograph.

"As I suspected," TR said, handing the picture to me.

"Patterson!"

"Who?" Brown asked. "What's going on?"

"Brownie, you have my deepest thanks and the knowledge that you have helped in a very grave crisis. There is even more I could ask you, but again you must assure me your lips will remain sealed."

"Is it really that important?"

"Absolutely vital," TR said solemnly.

"All right, shoot."

TR told Brown to prepare detailed background reports on Hooke and Crittenden.

"I have already picked up some rumors from our Washington reporter," Brown said. "I hear that Hooke might run against you, with Crittenden providing financial backing. Is this a political thing you're getting me involved in?"

"In a way, yes," TR said. "But I give you my word as a gentlemen that base political ambitions are not my motivation. I cannot divulge the reason."

Brown nodded with a smug smile, as if he didn't really believe the president, but he'd go along. He sighed and stood up. "So I leave the city with nothing more than a pat on the back?" he asked.

"Would an exclusive story make you feel better?" TR asked.

"It would."

"You may say, based on unnamed sources, that William Rufus

Day is looked upon with favor by the Administration to fill the Supreme Court vacancy created by the unfortunate passing of Associate Justice Gray."

"You mean you're nominating Day?" Brown asked.

"The rest of the world will learn about it tomorrow. You are the first outside of my inner circle to hear of it."

"Well, it's not as newsworthy as Tammany Hall unveiling a new statue, but I suppose it will have to do," Brown said grumpily.

TR harrumphed and took off his glasses. "All right then, I have a second story, which you must hold for a couple of days. It involves the coal strike."

Brown took out his notebook.

"You can report that sources in the White House said President Roosevelt and Attorney General Knox met to discuss the feasibility of bringing an antitrust action against the big coal operators in the event the coal strike continues much longer."

"Wow!" Brown said, jotting feverishly. "Will you do it?"

"That remains to be seen," TR said.

"One quick question. Will you run again?"

"I have not yet made up my mind."

"That would be a fine exclusive," Brown said hungrily.

The president buffed his glasses. "Brownie, word of caution. Hooke and Crittenden are dangerous men. If you make inquiries, do so with delicacy."

"I'm one of the most delicate chaps in the business," Brown said. "Maybe the best thing would be a little publicity. It would make them—"

"No!" TR thundered, cutting the newsman off. "I have spoken to you as a friend asking a favor, as well as the chief executive. You will *not* let anyone know about this."

"I understand," Brown said.

TR shook his hand. "One day, you can tell your grandchildren you did a great deed for your country."

Brown nodded and took a few steps toward the door. "Perhaps you might recommend some establishments where there are generous drinks and loose-talking officials?"

"I am sure Mr. White can help you along those lines," TR said.

I walked Brown out, giving him the names of several taverns. When I came back, TR was sitting with his eyes closed.

"I don't understand why you gave Brown that story on the coal strike," I said.

"With few exceptions, newspaper people are different from you or me," he said. "They crave tidbits of information the way most men do food. They can be nuisances, bores, and troublemakers, but this country would not be as great as it is without their meddlesome yattering."

"Will you be bringing an antitrust action against the coal-mine owners?"

TR chuckled, removed his glasses, and buffed them contentedly. "Knox and I have decided to wait and see what the courts rule on the cases against Northern Securities and Swift. But an item in the *World,* following Brownie's exclusive on the Day appointment, should make Baer and his cronies sweat."

"Then it isn't true?"

"It most certainly is. Knox and I discussed the matter. I did not tell Brown my decision, and he probably would not care if I did."

"If you don't mind my asking, why didn't you check out this information with Burnson?"

"He's a good and honest officer, but no longer a field man. For him to do anything would mean involving others, and I'm afraid there aren't many I trust in law enforcement. Sometimes you might not understand my actions, but know that they are always in the country's interests."

"I never had any question about that, sir."

A couple of days later, things began to pop.

TR had ordered up failed assassin William Heinz's personnel records but they were reported destroyed. I went over, flirted with a few clerks, bandied about the president's name, and found a back-up copy. The most interesting entry in the file was Heinz's main reference—Marlowe, the head of the presidential security detail.

TR was chewing on that piece of news when word came that the Kaiser was recalling Baron von Holleben to Germany. He replaced him with Speck von Sternberg, an old buddy of TR's. A sharp move by the Kaiser, since TR was going to be arbitrator on the Venezuala dispute.

Then the *World* ran the coal-strike story TR had planted, and Republican boss Marcus Alonzo Hanna stopped by.

"Is this true?" Hanna asked, waving a copy of the paper.

"I have discussed it with Mr. Knox," the president said.

"I hope it's not necessary."

"I will not allow millions of Americans to freeze because a gang of mine operators are worried about the extent of their profits," TR said, biting into each word like a child attacking a licorice whip. "The prime necessity is saving the people from a fearful calamity."

"I will see what I can do," Hanna said.

"I never thought of you as a champion of the working man," TR said. "I would have thought you would like to see the union broken."

"If the furnaces are not stoked, the steel mills do not run, and the trains do not transport."

"Your concern for the common man does my heart good," TR said.

"I want you to know that you may call on us at any time you need us," Hanna said. "We want to keep the country running smoothly as much as you do."

"I am sure the American people would be glad to hear that," TR said.

Hanna rose stiffly, the two men shook hands, and the Republican power broker left.

TR limped briskly around the office.

"The nerve of that man, talking like you would need his help," I said.

"I may just, Jim, I may just. The robber barons can move far quicker than the government, which is bound to act within the bounds of propriety." He limped over to the window and looked out. "The trees are losing their leaves. Winter is approaching. I can see the families huddled in their tenements and ramshackle farm houses, turning blue as the freezing wind dances and George Baer preaches his selfish gospel." He sighed.

"Do you realize what that little visit meant?" TR asked after a long pause.

I shook my head.

"That Hanna will not challenge me for the presidency next year."

"What makes you say that?"

"I understand the politician's mind and language. He is telling me he believes he can work with me, if I work with him. The question is, do I want to?"

"They know you can win, so they will fall in behind you."

There was a knock at the door. I got up, my hand resting on the butt of my revolver. I knew assassins didn't generally knock, but my nerves became frayed every time I thought of Lincoln, or Garfield, or McKinley. In the past forty years, three presidents had been felled by assassins' bullets. These are violent times we live in.

I threw the door open and a surprised Ike Hoover stared at me. "Mr. Brown is most insistent on seeing you."

"I've gathered quite a bit of information. I sense a spectacular story," Brown said, when we let him in. "If we were to run this in an Extra issue edition, it would——"

"Sell out, no doubt. And make the American people most restless. And give crackpots and fanatics ideas. No, Brownie, your only reward will be knowing that you served your country well."

We rang the bell for service, and Audrey came. Her eyes met mine and I felt their magnetism. We ordered coffee and pastries.

"Still carrying a torch for her?" TR asked after she left the room.

"The flame has burned out," I responded.

"If there is no spark there, then I will eat my Rough Rider hat."

I must have blushed for the men grinned at me. When she returned with our order, TR said, "Jim was just asking if you could have off this Friday so that you might go riding in Rock Creek Park with him."

Audrey looked at me.

"I—I—I did not do——" I said.

"If Mrs. Roosevelt has no objections, I think a little time in the outdoors might do you both good," the president said to her, cutting me off.

"Thank you, Mr. President," she said, with a polite curtsy. She hurried from the room without looking back.

"It is time you started thinking about settling down," TR said. "You could do far worse than Audrey McFarlane." Then the president put a half dozen lumps of sugar in his oversized coffee cup, took a bite from the warm apple turnover, and we began.

Brown laid out a bunch of clippings and a few pages of notes. There really wasn't anything besides background information, but TR took it all down, thanked the newsman, and dismissed him.

After Brown had left, we set to work, TR reading off names, me drawing lines and boxes. When we were finished, TR studied the chart. "Alarming, most alarming. Look at this motley crew," he said. "A robber baron eligible for membership in the Four Hundred, a United States senator, a master criminal, an officer in the Secret Service, a Secret Serviceman of German descent, a Colombian pimp and his prostitute, members of a traveling entertainment company, and a group of Tammany strong-arms."

"A coalition," I said.

"Exactly. I fear the worst—that all of these forces have united to topple me."

"We could call out the Army, round them all up in one fell swoop," I suggested.

"The public would see it as the act of a dictator," Roosevelt said. "I couldn't blame them. The newspapers in my enemies' hands would fan the flames. Besides, if they were able to infiltrate my own Praetorian guard, who is to say the armed forces are free of contamination?"

"What can we do?"

TR leaned back and buffed his glasses.

"The only defense that is worth anything is the offensive," he said.

sixteen

"What did you have in mind?" I asked.

"We shall go undercover again to find out the status of their plan. I want to see how widespread it is in Washington."

"It will be too easy for someone to recognize you here," I said. "I can go alone, or maybe get—"

He slammed his fist down on the desk. "Poppycock! I am not an armchair commander. When those blackguards stole from the ranch, I did not dispatch the hands after them while I warmed myself by the fire. When Kettle Hill had to be taken, I did not say, 'Forward, men,' and sit back. In this crisis, I will not shirk my duty. It is time for manly action."

"Mr. President, I really think it is better for you to . . ."

Needless to say, I did not sway him one whit. But time was on my side.

The fifty-eighth session of Congress was about to begin and there was a flurry of activity over at the Capitol Building. I hoped that with all this going on—including several spectacular receptions thrown by congressmen eager to make friends before the session began—TR would forget his plan.

All the whooping and hollering meant more work for me and

the Rough Riders. By the time Friday rolled around, I was as happy as a clam to get away from the White House. Before I left I made sure that my watchdog duties were taken over by two of the most trusted Rough Riders.

Audrey and I picked up our mounts from the stable. It was an Indian summer day, and painfully clear that the nation's capitol had been built on a swamp. Our clothes clung damply and mosquitoes the size of red-tailed hawks preyed on us. We went riding in Rock Creek Park and our conversation was as lifeless as the limp flags along Embassy Row.

As we neared Dumbarton Oaks, she spurred her brindle filly and took off at a gallop. My bay gelding couldn't keep up. It was several miles before we were together again, but the air rushing by had refreshed us and wiped clean the slate.

We tethered the horses and walked to the creek. I pulled my boots off, rolled my pants up, and stepped into the cool water. She made sure no strangers were around, hiked her skirt above her knees, and joined me.

"I am sorry I ever doubted you," she said, and we kissed.

"I am sorry I gave you reason to," I said, and we kissed again.

We walked with the horses. There was much hand-holding and pausing to hug. I felt like a trail hand home with his bride after a long cattle drive.

"I love you," I said.

"I love you too."

My adventures with Mr. Roosevelt had been getting me down. We spoke guardedly about my helping the president.

"I don't like it," she said. "Why won't he let the Secret Service or the Army or the police take care of it?"

"The full story of what's been going on would hurt TR and the whole country. As president, he can't afford even a hint of scandal. The sidewinders have been too clever. We are not even sure how widespread it is. If we go barreling in, we might not get the whole kit and caboodle."

"It still seems to me a large police agency would be better equipped to handle the matter."

"He doesn't know who to trust."

"So he calls you and the Rough Riders in. How long will this go on? Can't you talk him into getting more help?"

"Don't forget who you're talking about. Theodore Roosevelt believes in fighting the good fight and not just being a bystander cheering others on."

"And you?" she asked, unconvinced.

"I believe in him. No one's like Mr. Roosevelt."

"You really care about him?"

"I do."

"Then I would try and convince him to leave this dirty work to others. I have a premonition about it."

I laughed and tried to hug her, but she pulled away.

"Do not scoff at me, James White. I've known him longer than you. The president can be a little boy at times. He's constantly testing himself and his companions. He has been fortunate so far. I pray that his good luck continues."

It was hard to frolic after such a serious speech. We returned to the White House.

I hoped that the president had forgotten his scheme, but after a few days he took me aside and said, "The time has come to utilize those Washington underworld contacts you wisely developed."

And so it was I found myself that night sneaking out the service entrance on the east side of the White House accompanied by a fat, bearded man with slicked black hair, black eyeglasses, and a bashed derby. I had a similar hat, along with a bushy handlebar mustache and muttonchops. As we stepped through the doorway, we nearly bumped into Audrey, who was leaning against a column and enjoying the night air. She looked at us strangely, started to say something, then turned away.

The cool night air carried faint smells of honeysuckle and jasmine. I wished I could have stayed with her on the portico. I thought of spending the rest of my life with her. The idea was real pleasurable.

"Bully," TR said as we continued on our way. "I do not think she knew who we were."

I just shook my head.

We walked up New York Avenue, then angled back onto Fourteenth Street at Thomas Circle. The street lamps cast long, flickery shadows. The people we passed were silent, hats pulled low on their faces, moving with a slow shuffle. The air was thick, like we were walking through a gloomy cloud. TR tried to break the mood by whistling "A Hot Time in the Old Town Tonight," but the tune died on his lips.

It reminded me of a time in the Rockies when the woods suddenly had gotten quiet. The hairs on the back of my neck had stood on end as I moved cautiously through the underbrush. I nearly stumbled over a mother grizzly guarding her cubs. I looked at her, she looked at me. I took off like a pronghorn. Luckily, she stayed with her cubs. Those same hairs were on end as we walked down the street.

It began to get noisier and more crowded. From saloons came the sound of tinkly pianos, mixed with men's voices and women's laughter. We came upon a dead horse lying in the street. The owner was kicking the obviously lifeless beast, until suddenly he broke into tears and lifted the animal's head in his arms.

"I don't have a good feeling about this," I whispered to TR. "Let's go back, Mr. President."

"Call me Moose," he answered. "Which is the bar where they were speaking against me?"

"Another block."

He moved quickly with the barest trace of a limp.

It was the biggest and loudest honky-tonk on the block. TR pushed through the swinging wooden doors. No one paid attention as we made our way to the bar. I ordered beers, and we turned so we could face the room. Overhead fans stirred the cigar-smoke-filled air and the gaslights trembled from the breeze. The walls were covered with a flocked red wallpaper. There was a long bar, with a tarnished brass footrail and seldom-emptied spittoons. Behind the bar was a smokey mirror and four shelves for John Barleycorn. The crowd was whooping it up.

"So where did you hear the speaker?" TR asked.

I looked toward where I remembered the entrance to the back room. There were four heavy doors, all alike, and all closed. "It's one of those," I said.

"Which one?"

I scratched my head. "I'm not sure."

We couldn't go over and just try them. From a chair tilted back and leaning against the wall, a big man with a huge jaw was keeping his eyes on the crowd. A wobbly gent walked to a door on the far right. The guard got up, questioned him, and then opened the door. Inside we could see a group of men seated and listening to a speaker. Because of the noise in the bar, we couldn't hear what the speaker was saying.

I spotted several people I recognized from my days and nights of debauchery. Griselda was flirting with a soldier. He pushed her off and she said something rude. She came toward us.

"I have an idea," I said to the president. I winked at Griselda and she practically ran to me. Her hair was messed up, her makeup had run, and she smelled of liquor.

"Would you beat that bum up for me?" she asked, indicating the military man.

"It's me, Jim," I said.

"Jimmy!" she said, grinding her hips against me. "But why the whiskers?"

"Uh, it's my wife. She's having me followed. It's hard for me to get out."

"Poor baby. That night you spent with me was the best I have had in ages. What say we do it again?"

Out of the corner of my eye, I could see the president. He was aghast and agape.

She pressed against me. "Ooooh, what's this?" She reached in until her hand was around my Colt. "You weren't carrying a gun the last time."

"Griselda, please."

"Griselda it is now. I thought it was Grissy-poo."

"Griselda, don't embarass me in front of my friend. Moose, I would like you to meet Griselda."

"A pleasure," TR said in a raspy voice.

"Oooooh, such a nice big gentleman," she said, turning her attention to him without missing a beat. "Would the two of you like to come back to my apartment and enjoy a little Southern hospitality? Or I could have a girlfriend join us."

"Maybe later," I said, as she reached into the president's vest pocket and toyed with his gold watch.

"You have the time," she said, tugging playfully at the chain.

"Grissy, Moose is politically oriented. I remember hearing a very exciting speaker here one night."

"You were so tipsy, you could have listened to a hack driver's horse whinny and thought it was Theodore Roosevelt hisself," she said.

TR smiled, which Griselda took as encouragement. She pressed against him. "You don't really want to listen to boring speeches when I can make you forget about politics, do you?"

The smile was replaced by an awkward grin as TR tried to pull away and found himself pinned against the bar by female flesh.

"Maybe later, Grissy. Do you know which door leads to the radicals' meeting room?"

"Sure."

"Which one?"

Her tongue flicked briefly across her lips, like a prairie rattler tasting the air at the mouth of a gopher burrow. She rubbed her thumb and index finger together.

"For five dollars, will you get us in there?" I asked.

She nodded. I took out the money and gave it to her. It disappeared into her bodice. "Last chance to come to my place. I'll credit the five-spot toward the night."

TR shook his head adamantly.

"Suit yourself," she said, fluffing her skirt and walking to the back.

The guard got up as he saw us approach.

"It's okay, Billy, these fellas are friends of mine. They'd rather spend the time listening to speeches than being with me."

"Must be idiots."

TR and I just smiled.

"Go ahead in," he said, indicating the second door from the right.

"I thought it was this one," I whispered to TR.

"You must have done quite a job undercover," Mr. Roosevelt said. "Do you think you will be seeing that woman again."

"I hope not. Why?"

"She stole my watch."

There were three dozen men of all shapes and sizes crammed into a room that was meant to hold no more than twenty. The lights were dimmed and a haze of smoke as thick as a storm cloud hung over the room. On the walls were paintings of scantily clad women partially covered by large banners for the Radical Workers Party.

A play was in progress on a small stage and I thought we had been directed to the wrong room. Then I saw who the villain was—a chubby, sloppy man wearing glasses and a mustache that made him look like Mr. Roosevelt. He had a voice like chalk on a blackboard and a mean laugh that sounded like a donkey's bray. I couldn't see the real Mr. Roosevelt's reaction in the darkness.

In the crude melodrama, the hero's daughter was forced into prostitution after the villainous "Mr. Roosevelt" made a deal with some bankers. Exactly how the events tied together made no sense, but the audience didn't care. They booed and hissed every time "Mr. Roosevelt" appeared. When the hero finally gave him a thrashing, the crowd clapped and stomped its feet.

A fat fellow with a sharp widow's peak came out when the lights went on. I remembered him vaguely from my drunken adventure. He took a sip from a glass of water on the lectern. He said his name was Kaye and that he hoped we had enjoyed the show.

"Brothers, you are aware of the great struggle against the railroad tyrants," he said. "The tyrants try to silence us by sending us to jail, but the American Railway Union only grows stronger. Think of the coal miners. Many were buried alive by their bosses when they spoke up against the horrible conditions in the bowels of the earth.

"The time for peaceful protest is fast passing. We need men willing to do battle as viciously and violently as the villains in their mansions and ivory towers. Industrial workers must unite, tear down the palaces of their oppressors, oust the treacherous Roosevelt from the White House, and take over the country, which is rightfully ours."

I looked over at TR. He was listening intently. I had seen the same look on his face when he was studying a tough problem.

"Our good work cannot progress without your help. Give us

your time, your energy. For those who can afford it, your hard-earned wages. It is an investment in your future, for yourself and your children. Do you want a forty-hour work week?"

"Yeah!" the crowd cheered.

"And no more long hard hours for your young sons and daughters, barely out of their mothers' arms?"

"Yeah!" they roared, and many stomped their feet.

"Make those greedy bastard millionaires responsible for the evils they cause. Brother Horton, come up please."

A stocky, late-middle-aged man in a dark overcoat got up from the front row and stood beside the speaker on the platform. He was missing his right arm.

"Brother Horton here worked for the Union Pacific as a brake man. One day, the brakes failed while he was uncoupling a freight. What did the minions of Edward Henry Harriman do? They fired Brother Horton two days before Christmas as he lay in his hospital bed."

There were boos and hisses.

"Three small children and a wife to support, no coal in the bin, no food in the cupboard," Kaye continued, as Horton nodded. If Harriman had walked in, he would have been torn asunder. I glanced over at TR. He was staring at Horton.

"For Brother Horton's good, for the good of workingmen across the country, of farmers who have their land stolen, of wives widowed by blast furnaces, of coal miners lost in the bowels of the earth, we must fight, fight, fight!"

Everyone was on their feet cheering. I felt a pang in my heart for poor Mr. Horton.

"The Amazing Amusement and Mystifying Performance Repertory Company and Road Show, Limited," TR said, loud enough for the man next to us to look over, and then move away like TR was a lunatic.

"Horton. He was in the crowd that chased us after the incident with Grace and Zach. Only then he had both arms," TR said.

"Are you sure?"

He looked at me indignantly. "I would not say it if I weren't."

The audience was draining out a side door. Many were dropping small coins into a box next to Horton, others were signing a roster Kaye held.

"What is the list for?" I asked.

"A list of men who are willing to give time for the cause," Kaye said. His burning eyes locked on me.

"What do you need done?" I asked.

"To go door-to-door and make others aware of our platform. As the presidential campaign nears there'll be more work."

A drippy-nosed man from the audience came over and tried to get Horton to give him some of the money he'd collected. Kaye grabbed the man by the scruff of the neck and dragged him outside. I sidled over to where TR was talking to Horton. "I used to work for the Union Pacific," the president claimed in a raspy voice. "I was a fireman on the Newark-to-Washington route."

Horton nodded.

"Did you ever work a Sonoma? It's a four-four-oh, with forty two-inch driving wheels and a coal tender. A beautiful piece of work."

"You're right there, brother."

"Well, there is no such thing. The Sonoma is a narrow-gauge wood burner. The Pennsylvania Railroad has the Newark-to-Washington, D.C., route."

"Oh yeah?" Horton sneered. "You want to make something of it?"

"No need to get hot under the collar. I recall you from a show I once saw you in. I admired your performance. Then and now."

"Oh yeah?" he asked.

"Don't worry about me causing a ruckus. I support your work. I would not be here if I didn't. I understand that the truth might have to get bent to further the cause. The world will be better once the moneymongers are tossed."

"Death to them all," I chimed in.

"Yes," TR said. "The gentleman speaking tonight was quite a talker. My friend and I wish we had money to contribute to the cause."

"If you cannot give money, how about time?" Horton asked.

"Anything to get that villain, Roosevelt, out of the White House," TR said. "I'd kill him myself if I had the chance."

The speaker had finished with the beggar. "Why don't you introduce me to your friends?" Kaye said to Horton.

"I don't know their names but they have the spirit."

I introduced myself as Jim Dakota; TR used the name Moose.

"Pleased to meet you both," Kaye said, pumping our hands. "Are you interested in the cause?"

We nodded.

"How interested?"

"I would do whatever I could to see the working man throw off his shackles," TR rasped. "Of course getting a fair share for me and mine."

Kaye looked around. The room had emptied and we were alone with him and Horton. "Would you like to go to another meeting?"

TR smashed his fist into his hand and it made a loud crack. "Meetings are okay, but me and my buddy are men of action. We will have to find our own way of righting the wrongs, I guess."

"Come with us," Kaye said confidentially. "You'll be very interested in what we have to say."

We exited the saloon, with me and Horton talking like old friends, and TR doing the same with Kaye. From the little dribs and drabs I heard, TR was spitting back what Kaye had said, and the public speaker was lapping it up.

Kaye had a carriage waiting a few blocks away. It was a showy vehicle, with two well-groomed horses and a tough-looking coachman.

"I must ask you gentlemen to tie these on," he said, giving TR and me silk handkerchiefs.

"I don't like being blindfolded," I said, but TR was already removing his glasses and putting the handkerchief in place. I was forced to go along with him.

How long we rode and in what direction, I can't say. I tried peeking, but it was useless. I felt many turns, rocking from side to side and bumping into the president, who was on the plushly upholstered seat next to me. At last, the carriage halted and we were led from it, up three steps and into a house.

"You may remove your blindfolds," Kaye said, and I tore mine from my face. We were in the main room of an elegant house. The furniture was the fancy stuffed kind I'd expect to find on a prosperous plantation. Chandeliers as big as the ones in the White House hung from gold-leafed ceilings. Seats were set up facing a platform raised a foot off the parquet floor.

What I saw on the stage chilled and thrilled me simultaneously. Standing behind the podium, big as life, was Spike. He was smoking a cigarette in a long silver holder, with a matching cane at his side, and a diamond stickpin on the front of his ruffled shirt. Sitting next to him, looking up and nodding along with his every word, was Grace.

TR and me slid into a pair of vacant seats in the third row.

". . . the glory days of the old South, before the War Between the States, and its disastrous outcome," Spike was saying. His voice was strong and silky smooth. The slight Boston accent he'd had when he'd visited Sagamore Hill was replaced by a Mississippi drawl. "So who comes along and throws gasoline on the fire? Mr. Theodore Roosevelt. He's not even in the White House for six months and he invites a nigra. To the White House. The *White* House!"

The audience grumbled. I patted my mustache, afraid that the glue would give because of the beads of sweat.

"When he didn't shoot that crippled black bear in Mississippi, the cheating, conniving Yankee carpetbagger plotted with the Northern press to make it a racial issue," Spike continued.

I didn't see any way out. There were a dozen thugs in the audience, four shotgun-toting guards who stood at the corners of the room, as well as Kaye and Horton. Horton had removed the sling that had held his arm pressed tightly against his side. He was no more handicapped than I. To add to our predicament, the giant Zach and tattooed Daley were among the guards.

Then the bottom really dropped out. Sitting right in front of us was Marlowe. My hand went from patting my mustache to the gun under my jacket. I wished it had more than six shots.

"What do we do?" I whispered to TR, as Spike called for a revolution.

"Watch and wait," TR said confidently.

"You men will be the fathers of a new America, a pure America," Spike was saying. "A hundred years from now, your names will be memorized by school children, the way Washington, Jefferson, and General Lee are honored today."

The bored cutthroats around us didn't care about being immortalized in textbooks. They were getting restless. In all my time in rough-and-tumble saloons, I had never seen a meaner collection of scars, broken noses, missing teeth, cruel lips, and vicious eyes. I felt like a babe in the woods.

I heard an ox with long greasy hair complaining to the man next to him. "Shut up!" Spike yelled, slamming his cane down on the table. The men jumped. Spike hopped down of the stage and walked over to the complainer, idly twirling the cane. With a sudden movement, he twisted the walking stick and a long dagger appeared at the tip. It was at the ox's throat before he knew what was happening.

"You are very rude. I hate rudeness. If you want to live the rest of your life struggling for scraps, fine. But don't interfere with my plans. Do you understand me?"

"Yes, suh," the ox said.

Spike paced to the front of the room. There was no doubt in anyone's mind that he had nearly slit the man's throat. He had the audience's complete attention.

"The Army and police will be fighting in the streets, leaving no one to protect banks, museums, jewelry stores," Spike continued. "To fund our revolution, raids will be necessary. Every man will keep whatever he needs."

The redneck roughnecks murmured a chorus of "Yeahs."

"Women will be helpless, their men away fighting, when we ride through the streets like Quantrill's Raiders."

Grace looked uncomfortable. The audience was very aware of her. As she crossed her legs, the men smacked their lips and made lewd comments. Marlowe stared at her.

"The South will rise again!" Spike shouted. The men cheered and tossed hats in the air. Grace unfurled a cloth. Pictures of Jefferson Davis and General Robert E. Lee came into view. Some of the cutthroats looked like they would cry as Grace sang "Dixie," accompanied by Daley, who laid down his shotgun and stroked the keys of a piano.

"Roosevelt has said how much he admires Abraham Lincoln."

There were boos and hisses. Daley softly played "Dixie" in the background.

"Roosevelt must leave the presidency exactly the way Lincoln did," Spike said.

The crowd shouted "Hurrah!"

"Buck up, Jim," TR whispered, squeezing my arm.

"I will talk to each of you personally before you leave," Spike announced. He led Grace through a door behind the small stage. The guards' grips tightened on their shotguns. Two men from the front row were escorted in. The door was shut. After a few minutes, Grace led them out and brought a second pair in.

Daley answered requests, playing tunes that were popular south of the Mason-Dixon line. TR and I sang along, faking the words we didn't know.

Marlowe's turn came and he went into the room. He didn't see us. I sang the next song with enthusiasm.

As the last in, we were the last to be called. By the time Grace came for us, all the cutthroats had been dismissed, the piano rolled away, the banner taken down. The guards, however, remained alert.

Spike sat at a table, arms folded, a peaceful expression on his face. Grace was next to him, fanning herself slowly. The fan concealed much of her face.

"What are your names?" Spike asked.

"Jim Dakota," I said, fighting to keep the quiver from my voice.

"And Moose," TR rasped.

"Why are you here?"

"To get a piece of what is rightfully mine," TR said, talking out of the side of his mouth like a real desperado.

Grace asked us about our skills, like street fighting, horseback riding, public speaking, shooting, writing, setting fires, and making bombs.

"Horton confirmed you are good people," Spike said. "Where can we contact you?"

I gave the address of Griselda's hotel.

"Good. You may go now."

"Thank you," I said, relaxing.

"We're eager to serve," TR said. "When will you need us? What do we have to do? Most of all, how much do we get for it?"

I could feel my heart pounding from my boots to my sweaty brow. I hoped he had not gone too far.

"Fair questions. Roosevelt will no doubt be the Republican candidate for the presidency next year. At the last minute, he will either drop out, or be killed. Our group will be prepared. Senator Hooke will move to save the party. He will step into the slot."

"Sounds good," TR said. "What about us?"

"Those who help will be rewarded. Anyone who hurts us will be punished. Would you like to be governor somewhere?"

TR and I nodded along. "Anything we can do, just let us know," TR said.

"I appreciate that," Spike responded, a little too sweetly.

My neck hairs shot up as straight as corn stalks. One of the guards opened the door for us. I saw Kaye and Horton sitting in the front row. Their throats were slit from ear to ear, making it look like they each had a second gaping red mouth below their natural one.

Before we could react, shotguns jabbed into our sides and our guns were taken.

Spike ripped the beard from TR's face. "It's so nice to see you again, Mr. Roosevelt."

seventeen

As soon as we were tied up, Zach and Daley started pounding us. The other guards egged them on.

"No more," Spike ordered, and they stopped in mid-swing. Spike turned to TR. "I find this most distasteful. Your coming here forces me to change my plans. Dame Fortune has dropped a goose on my table. I have to decide how best to carve it." With a wave of his hand, he sent Zach, Daley, and the other guards away. Marlowe lingered, looking longingly at Grace.

"How could you betray the nation, betray me, like this?" TR asked him.

"When Spike takes over, *I* will be the secretary of the treasury," Marlowe said.

"That's right, Marlowe, now, please leave us alone," Grace said. The traitor left without looking back.

"He's in love with Grace and the scent of power," Spike said with a knowing smirk. "Perhaps he could resist one, but never both."

A candle was burning low on the table, the room was shuttered, and heavy curtains blocked the little light that slipped in.

"I must apologize for my minions," Spike said. "I abhor unnecessary violence, simplistic brutality." He was silent for a long time, gazing off into space. Grace tapped his shoulder, and he rejoined us.

"Uh, oh yes. Where was I, oh, I was deciding the best way to use your visit." He paused. "Why don't you try and reason with me, convince me not to harm you, offer me money, power, or glory?"

"I doubt that reasoning would work with you," TR said.

"You think I'm crazy? But it's you who are trussed like a piece of meat ready to be butchered. It's my empire on the rise and yours that's collapsing.

"Twice, I slipped through your defenses," he said with a sneer. "You try the same gambit with me, and fall right into my lap. Superior intelligence will triumph.

"My assault on the presidency is but further proof. I have kept tight control. It minimizes the possibility of betrayal, and maximizes the spoils. We have put together a syndicate of special interests, ranging from Tammany saloons to Southern plantations, from out-of-work socialists to mansion-owning moguls."

"'We' meaning you, Hooke, and Crittenden?" TR asked.

"Yes, those two. For now." Grace patted his arm, as if to say, "Be quiet," but he ignored her and glared at the president. "You arrogant, power-mad bastard. I'm going to show you what an orphan from the South Side of Chicago can do. Just like Crittenden, that tub of lard, who thought he had me under his thumb. He's learned his lesson."

"Won't you be sharing your kingdom with the other robber barons?" TR asked. His tone was relaxed, but I could hear a slight asthmatic wheeze.

Spike shook his head violently. "Those men are fools. They're afraid to rock the boat. As soon as you are gone, they will be too."

"You don't have a chance," I said. "Our security men are on their way."

"Mind your manners, cur, or I will turn the empress loose," he said, indicating the wet-lipped Grace. "You forget that I have Marlowe as a pipeline into your security. I know about the president's hobby of sneaking off without telling anyone." He turned to the president. "Mr. Theodore Roosevelt, hero to so many people. Look where he is now. Look at him. Look!" He seized the president's jaw, squeezed, and shook like a greenhorn on a bronco. Grace put her arms around him.

"It's okay, it's okay," she said soothingly.

He pulled away. "I'll send Zach to fetch Crittenden. He can witness the death of a president for a mere five hundred thousand dollars. A small price to pay, right, Empress?"

She gave him a peck on the cheek and the happy couple left the room. TR and I immediately began struggling against our bonds.

"I apologize for getting you into this," TR said.

"I was supposed to be protecting you."

"I only have to be concerned about this madman," TR said. "You must worry about Edith's wrath." He managed a smile and I tried to answer him with one.

"Can you topple your chair?" he asked.

"Probably."

"Can you do it so that the rope is near my face?"

"Possibly. But why?"

"Try it," he commanded.

I rocked back and forth, edging my chair close to the president's. Finally it fell over. I was half lying in the his lap, the back of my chair inches from his face. The famous presidential incisors went to work on my bonds.

I stared ahead in the darkness. There were footfalls outside the door. Whoever it was moved away. TR kept gnawing.

I felt a sharp tug and a rope fell free. I strained and another gave. I leapt from the chair and untied the president. The rough hemp had torn his lips.

We ran to the window. The shutters were painted metal, and barred. He went to the fireplace and selected two stout logs. "Prehistoric man felled mammoths and mastodons with as much," TR said encouragingly, handing me a club. "Surely we can do as well."

"But mammoths didn't have shotguns."

"Thank goodness or we might live on a planet ruled by the woolly beasts."

"What do we do now?"

"If we lure Spike into the room, we can take him hostage. If we only snare a guard, at least we'll get his gun."

It turned out we didn't need to try TR's desperate plan. Outside the house we heard shots fired.

"What's going on?" Spike shouted.

"We're being raided," Daley answered.

"Get the prisoners," Spike said.

TR pointed to a spot next to the door and blew out the candle. We were in total darkness. The door swung open and a pistol-toting Daley stepped into the room. I brought my club down as if my life depended on it. Because it did. Daley crumpled.

There were more shots. We could hear them ricocheting in the corridors. I scooped up Daley's gun. The cold steel felt good in my hands.

"What's happening?" Spike yelled from the front room.

Another villain came into our room. I conked him, preferring to save ammunition. TR took the second guard's gun.

I peeked out. Bullets winged through the front door. Spike and Grace were hiding behind pillars, both holding shotguns. Marlowe and a guard were swapping shots with unseen foes.

"Drop it!" I yelled, and they spun with guns blazing. Both TR and I emptied our guns at them. Marlowe and the guard took a one-way ride to Boot Hill. I saw Grace draw a bead on the president. Then a swarm of bullets stung the front door to bits and she fell.

"Grace!" Spike screamed, and dropped his gun. He threw himself on his fallen mistress and held her. More shots rattled through the door. Spike cradled the lifeless body. He chanted a nonsense song.

A voice I knew ordered, "Come out with your hands up!"

I never thought I'd be so happy to see the scowling face of General Leonard Wood, as he came through the door followed by Spider Monaghan and Bat Masterson.

Masterson locked a pair of handcuffs on Spike and left him ranting and raving in the front hall. We searched the house and found enough munitions to outfit a small army. All the cutthroats had either left before the shootout or escaped when they heard gunfire.

"But how in Hades did you know we were in trouble?" I asked when we were done thanking our rescuers.

"You can thank Miss McFarlane for that," Wood said. He explained how she had seen through our disguises. She had followed us to the saloon on Fourteenth Street, taking her life in her hands on that street of sin. Twice she had had to defend her honor with a hatpin. But she had called Wood. He and the others tailed us to Spike's retreat.

"The general and I were arguing about storming the fort, when the big bald cuss came out," Masterson said.

"Zach," I filled in.

"I wanted to talk to him, but he wanted to strangle me. I had to use an Arkansas toothpick to send him to his Maker," Masterson said. "We decided you fellas were up a creek without a paddle. So we reckoned we'd give you one."

"I'm confident the dead all have lengthy criminal records," Wood said. "If the police come and we aren't here, they will no doubt assume there was a falling out among thieves."

We looked to TR, who had been strangely quiet. "I would prefer not to tip my hand quite yet. May I borrow your matches?" he asked Monaghan, who had a stogie hanging from his lips. The Rough Rider handed it over.

"I believe you told me you investigated several arson cases?" TR asked me. "Let's get Zach's body inside and see if you are as good a criminal as you are a detective."

"I don't understand," I said.

"A fire will cover the cause of death, and keep Crittenden and Hooke off balance," TR explained. "They will not know whether Spike is alive. It will give me time to plan my attack."

I set the fire, using kerosene, a few of the gas lamps, and two candles as a timer. The house went up like a tinderbox. By the time the fire companies got there, not much more than the chimneys were standing. Our little group, with Spike gagged and bound, watched safely from a quarter mile away.

During the ride back, Wood examined Spike, who alternated between silence—during which he would glare at us—and ranting about how he would take over the world. Spittle dribbled from the corner of his mouth.

"The tertiary stage of syphillis, I think," Wood said, giving the madman a sedative. Spike's face, which had been twisted by his private demons, at last relaxed.

"The key to this conspiracy, and he has the sense of a loon," the president muttered as the horses clip-clopped down the road into the city.

Wood agreed to take Spike back to his house and care for him until the president decided what to do.

"We have captured only one-third of a very dangerous triumvirate," Mr. Roosevelt said after we dropped them off. "Crittenden is the linchpin, the man with the money. Hooke is weak and can be broken, but Crittenden . . ."

Mr. Roosevelt was upset. Me, I was glad to be alive. I leaned back and savored every bump and bounce.

A few White House staff members were still up and about at that late hour. We talked as if we were coming back from a reception, and fooled them. Audrey was waiting on the second floor, an anxious look on her face. She saw us and tried to look nonchalant.

"You have been a very naughty lady," TR said seriously. "And I do not think there is any way I can thank you enough. I will have to leave that to my associate." He gave a slight bow, and limped off, leaving the two of us alone.

"Are you okay?" she asked.

I kissed her.

"You are," she said, answering her own question.

I spent that night in her arms.

I got up in the early morning hours to return to my bed before anyone took notice.

I was startled when I passed near the portrait of Lincoln and saw TR pacing. I didn't speak for a few minutes. TR's jowls hung lower, his squint lines furrowed deeper, his hair seemed to have receded overnight.

"Is there anything I can do?" I finally asked.

"You have done all you can," he said. "You've been a fine friend and a good American." As he spoke, he looked at the painting, as if he were addressing Lincoln.

"Let us see to it that while we take advantage of every gentler and more humanizing tendency nowadays, we preserve the iron quality which made our predecessors triumph."

"Do you want to talk about it?"

He turned to face me. "I will need your assistance. We will

borrow a page from *Hamlet* and another from the laws of the wild, and devil take the hindmost. Have you heard of Jean Martin Charcot?"

I shook my head.

"He's a French physician who has done some remarkable work with asthma. As well as ataxia, the lack of coordination common in the final stages of syphillis. Anyway, Spike's condition reminded me of his work."

"I don't understand, sir."

"Charcot has also done pioneering work with mesmerism."

"Animal magnetism?"

"Exactly."

"But how does that help us with Crittenden and Hooke?"

With that, he told me his plan. It was both a brilliant and dangerous gamble, just the sort you'd expect from him.

Invitations were sent out for a dinner to be held at the White House in four days.

The state dining room had hosted kings, emperors, and the men who made our country tick, but never had so many tycoons been scheduled to dine under the same roof. Ronald Crittenden, J.P. Morgan, E.H. Harriman, Andrew Carnegie, Henry Clay Frick, John D. Rockefeller and his son were on the guest list. Senator Hooke and General Wood were also invited.

TR was a master at mixing up a collection of guests. With literary figures like Lincoln Steffens and Owen Wister, he would throw in a couple of diplomats, a prizefighter, and a senator. So it was not considered strange that I was joining these captains of industry and statesmen.

Audrey and I had little time for socializing. I was by Mr. Roosevelt's side constantly. She was busy helping Mrs. Roosevelt with the preparations. At last I had a few minutes off, and I cornered my beautiful maid by the stairwell.

"By the way, I didn't ask you what made you follow us?" I asked after enjoying a kiss.

"I had a feeling you and the president were getting into trouble."

"What if you had been wrong?"

"At worst, I would have lost my job."

There was no hint of the passion of the night before. Our words were cool, logical, like friends analyzing a chess game.

"What's your middle name?"

"Maureen. Why?"

"Audrey Maureen McFarlane, will you marry me?"

"I don't want you proposing merely as a way of showing your gratitude. I was concerned about the president too."

"Has he asked for your hand?"

"No."

"Good, then I repeat my offer. I love you for the way you walk, talk, think, breathe, kiss, and wade in the water."

"You don't know whether I can cook."

"Can you cook?"

"Yes."

"Then it's settled. Let's set the date for you to become Mrs. James White."

She pressed her lips to mine. "I thought you'd never ask," she said when we came up for air.

"Deee-lightful," TR bellowed, pumping my hand and giving Audrey a fatherly buss when he heard the news. It was his first smile since before the night at Spike's.

In the following days, I alternated between feeling like I was walking on air and worrying about what would happen at the big dinner.

eighteen

"How do I look?" I asked Audrey, as I stood before her dressed in a black tuxedo.

"Turn around," she told me. Obeying was easy, like we were an old married couple. Even having her in my room wasn't unnatural, though of course we left the door open.

"You look wonderful," she said, removing a bit of fluff from my jacket.

"Not as wonderful as you," I said, embracing her.

Mrs. Roosevelt cleared her throat from the doorway and I quickly released Audrey. "She was just helping me . . ."

The First Lady smiled. "No need to explain what she was helping you with. Audrey, when you are free, Annie could use your assistance in the kitchen. The catering people are proving impossible to deal with."

"Very good, ma'am," McFarlane said, with a hint of a curtsey. As soon as Mrs. Roosevelt was gone, Audrey gave me a playful slap. "There you go, getting me in trouble."

"I'll really get you in trouble if you don't watch out," I said, reaching for her.

She scooted out the door, then turned back and looked at me seriously. "What's going to happen tonight?" she asked.

"Keep your fingers crossed," was all I told her.

As soon as she was gone, I went to the dresser, removed a derringer and a blackjack. I tucked both items under my vest.

The room was as tense as a saloon right before a gunfight. This time it wasn't a faro cheater being called out. The fate of the country hung on how TR played his hand.

I walked in trying to be casual and found my seat. To my right was Senator Hooke, and to my left was none other than J.P. Morgan. Across the table from me sat Crittenden.

Morgan had an appetite as big as his financial holdings. He had seconds and thirds on everything. Food disappeared from his plate.

Carnegie was a much smaller man, with the tough, energetic movements of a bantamweight boxer. He was a fast eater. After gulping his portion down, he stared at us, drumming his fingers on the table.

Rockefeller Sr. looked like a skinny old monkey picking at his food. The son followed his father's example.

Coke-and-coal tycoon Frick—slightly built, with pale, delicate features—sat silently next to Carnegie. The men had done millions of dollars of business with each other, but you wouldn't know it from the way they acted. They must've had some sort of squabble.

Harriman had the piercing eyes and high forehead of an intellectual. He savored every morsel of food as if he were going to give a gourmet critique.

Crittenden, the jolly fat man, ate heartily and without much regard for manners. He must've thought he was in the clear, with Spike apparently dead and gone. I overheard him telling Harriman a lewd story involving a traveling salesman and a farmer's immoral daughter: Harriman laughed so hard he gagged on a piece of meat.

Although their looks were different, they were brothers under the skin. They would crush anyone or anything that got in their way. Presidents come and go, but money is forever.

There were two empty seats at the table, one next to Crittenden, the other by my neighbor Hooke.

The meal began with *croûtes panaches* and went on to *potage consommé printanier aux quenelles de volaille* and *tartalettes à la Moelle*. The caterer gave dishes a French name so he could charge more.

The wine flowed and everyone relaxed. Crittenden and Frick were debating the best place to vacation in Europe. Carnegie and Harriman were chatting. J.P. and I were yakking about the game called basketball, which was catching on fast.

"Who's missing the meal?" Rockefeller asked in a crotchety voice, pointing to the empty seats with a hand like a skeleton.

"Dr. Wood is bringing a guest. They should be here very shortly," TR said chummily. A few minutes later, Wood entered with the final guest. Spike moved slowly, with the glazed eyes of the mesmerized.

"Oh my God!" Hooke said, pulling back from the table and spilling his dish on the floor. I had dropped my silverware at the sudden movement and reached under my jacket to grasp the blackjack.

"My friend Spike has an interesting story to tell," Wood said.

"Don't believe a word of it," Hooke shouted. "It's a lie. A vicious lie."

"Shut up, you cretin," Crittenden hissed. "They cannot prove a thing."

The others at the table were intrigued.

Wood led Spike to his seat. "You must excuse Spike," Wood said. "He's had a long journey. That's why we were late in getting here. I hope we haven't missed anything."

"It's party time," Spike said cheerily. "President Hooke. Mr. Crittenden. I told you we'd be in the White House."

"You know these gentlemen?" TR asked, feigning surprise.

"It's a lie, a vile, vicious lie," Hooke insisted.

Crittenden's eyes shifted from side to side, searching for the exits. Wood and I were placed so he couldn't run without passing by us.

"President Hooke, I deserve more money," Spike said. "It was I who got rid of that fat fool, Roosevelt."

TR looked offended and set down the piece of bread he'd been eating.

"We made the deal. Crittenden paid me, you were supposed to give me more money and patronage positions to dispense," Spike complained.

Hooke snatched the knife from the table and lunged to silence Spike. My blackjack caught him on the wrist. The blade fell. His chest heaved with hatred, as Spike looked on with vacant eyes. The robber barons watched. They had stopped eating, except Morgan, who was cleaning his plate. The captains of industry were enjoying the drama.

Crittenden rose and tossed down his napkin. "I do not have time for your little playlet," he said. "You must excuse me."

"You don't want to hear what Spike has to say?" TR asked.

"I certainly do not," Crittenden said. "Good night."

I looked at TR, unsure how to act. The president waved his hand. "Have a good night, Mr. Crittenden. I know I shall."

Crittenden hurried out.

"I don't have to listen either," Hooke said shrilly.

"No, you don't. Perhaps you already know what Spike has to say?"

"I, I, I . . ." Hooke sputtered.

"Mr. White, would you show Senator Hooke out."

I led the senator from the room. General Wood followed us and escorted his confused charge off into the night. I returned to the State Dining Room and locked the door. The robber barons were murmuring and mumbling. TR rose slowly and they quieted down.

"Gentlemen, what I am about to say to you is a matter of the utmost importance and confidentiality," TR said. "If details were to escape this room there would be dire consequences.

"The man, Spike, was acting in the employ of Senator Hooke and Mr. Crittenden in a plot to oust me from the presidency and take over the country," TR said, biting into each word with vigor.

I expected gasps or shocked exclamations, but the moguls kept poker faces.

"Crittenden provided the brains and the financial backing, Hooke was the respectable puppet, and Spike the underworld operator who supplied the manpower. There are others, but they're relatively powerless without the prime movers."

As he spoke the president's eyes moved from face to face, burning in his message. He focused on Rockefeller. "If this country is plunged into anarchy by their short-sighted manipulations, your oil wells will not be worth a bottle of snake oil. Entire fields will burn."

The president locked eyes with Harriman. "The railroads are particularly vulnerable, stretched out for thousands of unsupervised miles. Can you protect all of them?"

He turned to Frick. "As rich as you are, you are all mortal. I need not go into the anarchists' near fatal attempt on your life following the strike at the Pennsylvania steel plant you share with Carnegie.

"Carnegie, you will profit for a while. Steel is always needed to make guns and knives during a rebellion. But what will you do when those weapons are turned on you and yours?"

"No one would dare," Carnegie said cockily.

TR took off his glasses and buffed. "Is even the House of Morgan safe when there is rioting in the streets?"

"You have made your foreboding predictions, Teddy," Morgan said impatiently.

"Then let me tell you something straight," TR said, smashing his fist on the table so that the silverware, and several of the guests, jumped. "The accident in Massachusetts was a deliberate attempt on my life. There have been other assaults, which I need not go into. It is a trade risk, which every prominent public man must accept as a matter of course.

"This conspiracy, however, exceeds the scope of any few fanatics getting together to rant into the wind and plan dire deeds. They have threatened to rend the very fabric of our civilization. They are the sort of malefactors of great wealth who cannot, and will not, be allowed to continue to prosper under our system.

"As you know, Congress recently passed my bill providing for the Department of Commerce and Labor."

There were hostile mumblings and grumblings around the table.

"Within that department will be the Bureau of Corporations to monitor and regulate the size of trusts. There will be a bible of new regulations to protect the public from voracious exploitation by companies grown too bloated for the national good."

Carnegie stood up. "Just because Crittenden stepped out of line is—"

"Lest any of you forget, I *am* the president," TR bellowed. "I'm not running a rival corporation. My stockholders are the American people, and I will do everything to see that they get a square deal."

"Did you invite us to dinner to tell us that?" Morgan asked.

"I wanted to make you aware of some of the resources that are available to me if I find myself encumbered at every step by big business," the president said. "The Northern Securities and the Swift and Company antitrust cases are the first of many. I'll make the Sherman Antitrust Act the most utilized legislation on the books."

"See how far that will get you," Harriman sneered.

The robber barons were on the edges of their seats. If they could've gotten away with killing the president right then, several would've tried.

"I tell you gentlemen, the big corporations must serve the public good or they will be destroyed. Dinosaurs once ruled the earth too. Now they are bones in a museum."

"You do not frighten us, Theodore Roosevelt," Carnegie said. "We will fight you in the courts, in the newspapers, in the streets if need be. You are not the only one who likes a good scrap."

TR folded his arms across his broad chest and let the silence grow. Carnegie fussed with his silverware. Morgan brushed his napkin across his mouth. The president waited until the robber barons were fidgeting like a bunch of boys on the last day of school.

"Our interests are really the same," TR said soothingly. "We want to see these United States move onward into the twentieth century and continue to be the greatest nation on earth.

"These scoundrels threaten to upset the applecart. If they are brought to trial, it will cause rumors of a conspiracy by the rich to take over the country. That will only provide fodder for the anarchists and radical socialists.

"I invited you gentleman here to show you that Crittenden and Hooke were conspiring," TR said in a level tone. "I'd like to resolve the matter as quickly as possible. In return for certain guarantees, I propose a one year moratorium on antitrust actions."

The president was not a gambling man, but he was bluffing as surely as the sharpest poker player. He'd told me secretly that there wasn't any point in filing any more lawsuits until the Northern Securities case was settled and a precedent was set, which was at least a year off. I laughed inside when I thought of what the robber barons would do if they knew what he was up to.

"You'll give us a chance to put our houses in order?" Morgan asked.

"You will have the time to work out suitable ways of preserving your businesses and adjusting them to fit within the framework of the law."

The tycoons leaned back in their seats and relaxed.

"In return, I want your help in crushing the conspiracy," TR said.

"While you and I have had our differences, the matter can be resolved in a civilized manner," Morgan said.

The others echoed him.

"What would you have us do?" Frick asked.

"I know people who can eliminate Hooke and Crittenden," Rockefeller said gleefully. "They handled that strike in—"

"I do not think that is what he means, Father," the younger Rockefeller interrupted.

"Oh," Rockefeller Senior said, slumping backward.

"I want Crittenden's fortune to disappear," TR said. "I don't have a specific method in mind, but I recall the free-market manipulations of Jay Gould, and remain confident that you gentlemen will be worthy of the task."

The multi-multi-millionaires bobbed their heads and smiled. Money looted from Crittenden would wind up in their vaults.

"Is that it?" Harriman asked suspiciously.

"No. I want you to give some of your money back to the people. Form foundations, build libraries, hospitals, parks—"

"What?" an outraged Frick interrupted.

"Tax benefits will accrue," TR said, throwing him a sharp glance. "It will improve your image and alleviate the burden on the public welfare system."

The robber barons reacted to the idea like a stallion with a burr under his saddle blanket.

"If the good Lord would have wanted to give these people charity, he would have done so Himself," Harriman said.

"I never knew you to be a religious man, Mr. Harriman," TR said. "Do you pray for new railroad routes, or rely on more earthbound approaches?"

The other robber barons chuckled and Harriman blushed.

"Let me remind you what it says in the Book of Matthew: 'It is easier for a camel to go through the eye of a needle than for a rich man to enter into the kingdom of God,'" TR said. "You are very rich men. You can take none of your wealth with you when you have shuffled off this mortal coil. An act of charity is a noble venture. And do not forget the tax advantages."

"I have thought about that," Carnegie said. "A foundation bearing my name and doing good work would be something I, and my children, and their children could point to proudly. You should all consider it for yourselves. Much as I hate to admit it, I think Roosevelt has a good idea."

"Bully. I don't ask for an immediate response. I do expect an answer within twenty-four hours. Mr. Morgan, will you act as spokesman for the group?"

"I shall."

"I leave for Sagamore Hill tomorrow. I can receive the answer there. Now, would anyone care for some of the most delicious pecan pie?"

The servants were called back, and pie and coffee were offered. Audrey was one of those serving, although it was not normally her chore during state dinners. She looked at me anxiously. I gave her a wink.

The wealthiest men in the world adjourned to the Red Room for sherry and cigars. They huddled in groups. TR and Edith talked in one corner, while I slipped over to Audrey.

"Did it work?" Audrey asked.

"I think so. It's part of Mr. Roosevelt's plan to let them have time to decide. It leaves them their dignity."

"Can you tell me now what his plan was?"

"The man behind TR's troubles, Crittenden, has been thrown to the chickens."

"What?"

"When a chicken is injured, the others in the barnyard peck it to death."

She had a puzzled expression.

"Crittenden is a chicken Mr. Roosevelt has injured," I explained. "It's up to the fowl to destroy him."

Morgan did not need to visit us at Sagamore. The answer came the next morning. The newspapers' business pages announced that Harriman was expanding his railroad operations in the northern United States to compete directly with Crittenden's lines.

Rockefeller and Frick dropped their oil and coke prices in markets where they competed with Crittenden. Carnegie canceled a major order he had with Crittenden for coal for his blast furnaces.

On Wall Street, large blocks of Crittenden's stock were dumped on the market and rumors spread. His creditors called in their loans. As details of his business setbacks became known, the rush to sell his stock turned into an avalanche. By day's end, Crittenden had less money than a saddle bum after a big Saturday night in town.

Crittenden's financial collapse was not the only shocking news. Senator David Hooke was found dead in his house, the victim of a self-inflicted gunshot wound.

TR made Bat Masterson the deputy U.S. Marshal for the Southern District of New York. The Tammany muscle men were tracked down and arrested on various outstanding warrants.

A couple of months later, Crittenden died of a stroke.

Six months after the conspiracy was crushed, Theodore Roosevelt was enthusiastically nominated for president at the Republican National Convention in Chicago. He went on to win reelection by the largest plurality ever.

TR never got his sight back in that eye. He let the public think he got it in a boxing accident. I always knew better. It was one heckuva sacrifice to make for our country, but I never heard him complain about it.

After turning down an offer to take charge of the Secret Service, I married Audrey and we moved to Denver. I thought I might be bored, but my beautiful bride kept me from getting itchy.

With the generous bonus/wedding present from the Roosevelts, we bought a few hundred acres and cattle and horses to graze on them.

I had a telephone installed, the first in the area. I knew that if there was trouble again, I would be getting a call.

bibliography

Blum, John Morton. *The Republican Roosevelt.* Cambridge, Mass.: Harvard University Press, 1954.

Connable, Alfred, and Silberfarb, Edward. *Tigers of Tammany.* New York: Holt, Rinehart and Winston, 1967.

Hagedorn, Hermann. *The Roosevelt Family of Sagamore Hill.* New York: Macmillan, 1954.

Hagedorn, Hermann, and Roth, Gary G. *Sagamore Hill: An Historical Guide.* Theodore Roosevelt Association, 1977.

Johnston, William Davison. *TR, Champion of the Strenuous Life.* Theodore Roosevelt Association, 1958.

Johnston, William Davison, editor. *The Words of Theodore Roosevelt.* Peter Pauper Press, 1970.

Josephson, Matthew. *The Robber Barons.* New York: Harcourt Brace and Company, 1934.

McCullough, David. *Mornings on Horseback.* New York: Simon & Schuster, 1981.

Morris, Edmund. *The Rise of Theodore Roosevelt.* New York: Coward, McCann & Geoghegan, 1980.

Morris, Sylvia Jukes. *Edith Kermit Roosevelt: Portrait of a First Lady.* New York: Coward, McCann & Geoghegan, 1980.

Pringle, Henry F. *Theodore Roosevelt: A Biography*. New York: Harcourt Brace and World, 1931.

Roosevelt, Theodore. *Letters from Theodore Roosevelt to Anna Roosevelt Cowles*. New York: Charles Scribner's Sons, 1924.

—————. *An Autobiography*. New York: Charles Scribner's Sons, 1926.

—————. *Theodore Roosevelt's Letters to His Children*. New York: Charles Scribner's Sons, 1926.

—————. *The Free Citizen*. Edited by Hermann Hagedorn. New York: Macmillan, 1956.

Teague, Michael. *Mrs. L: Conversations with Alice Roosevelt Longworth*. New York: Doubleday, 1981.

Time-Life editors. *This Fabulous Century 1900–1910*. New York: Time-Life Books, 1969.